# MIDNIGHT RESCUE

*Christy® of Cutter Gap*

# MIDNIGHT RESCUE

*Christy*
of Cutter Gap

THE SERIES

*Based on the novel* Christy *by*

## CATHERINE MARSHALL

EVERGREEN
FARM

an imprint of
GILEAD PUBLISHING

*Midnight Rescue*: The Christy® of Cutter Gap series
Adapted by C. Archer
Copyright © 1995 by Marshall-LeSourd, LLC

Published by Evergreen Farm, an imprint of Gilead Publishing, LLC,
Wheaton, Illinois, USA.
www.gileadpublishing.com/evergreenfarm

ISBN: 978-1-68370-173-6 (printed softcover)
ISBN: 978-1-68370-174-3 (ebook)

Cover design by Larry Taylor
Cover illustrations © Larry Taylor. All rights reserved.
Interior design by Beth Shagene
Ebook production by Book Genesis, Inc.

Printed in the United States of America.

18  19  20  21  22  23  24  /  5  4  3  2  1

# *The Characters*

**Christy Rudd Huddleston,** a nineteen-year-old girl

**Christy's Students:**
    **Rob Allen,** fourteen
    **Creed Allen,** nine
    **Little Burl Allen,** six
    **Bessie Coburn,** twelve
    **Lizette Holcombe,** fifteen
    **Wraight Holt,** seventeen
    **Mountie O'Teale,** ten
    **Ruby Mae Morrison,** thirteen
    **John Spencer,** fifteen
    **Lundy Taylor,** seventeen

**David Grantland,** the young minister

**Ida Grantland,** David's sister

**Alice Henderson,** a Quaker mission worker from
    Ardmore, Pennsylvania

**Dr. Neil MacNeill,** the physician of the Cove

**Jeb Spencer,** a mountain man

**Fairlight Spencer,** his wife
  (Parents of Christy's student John)

**Duggin Morrison,** stepfather of Ruby Mae Morrison

**Mrs. Morrison,** Ruby Mae's mother

**Tom McHone,** a mountain man

**Bird's-Eye Taylor,** feuder and moonshiner
  (Father of Christy's student, Lundy)

**Ben Pentland,** the mailman

**Jake Pentland,** Ben's nephew

**Elias Tuttle,** owner of the El Pano general store

**Bob Allen,** keeper of the mill by Blackberry Creek
  (Father of Christy's students, Rob, Creed, and Little
    Burl)

**Granny O'Teale,** great-grandmother of Christy's student,
  Mountie

**Jubal McSween,** a moonshiner

**Janey Cook,** a pregnant mountain woman

**Prince,** black stallion donated to the mission

**Goldie,** mare belonging to Miss Alice Henderson

**Lightning,** dapple-gray stallion belonging to Lundy Taylor

**Robert E. Lee,** chestnut mare belonging to Ben Pentland

**Possom,** bay gelding belonging to Elias Tuttle

**Pegasus (Peg),** piebald mare belonging to Rob Allen's
  father, Bob

**Old Theo,** crippled mule owned by the mission

**Bill,** Dr. MacNeill's horse

**Mabel,** one of the schoolhouse hogs

**Scalawag,** raccoon belonging to Creed Allen

# *One*

"MAY I HAVE THIS DANCE, MISS HUDDLESTON?"

Christy Huddleston grinned. "I have to warn you, David. I'm not a very good dancer."

"Then we'll make the perfect couple."

Christy joined David Grantland on the wide lawn in front of the mission house where she lived. David, the young mission minister, looked especially charming today. He was wearing his best suit, and his dark hair was slicked back neatly. Christy wore her favorite dress, made of bright yellow linen with crisp white lace down the bodice. In her braided, sun-streaked hair she wore a matching yellow bow.

Today, Saturday, April 6, 1912, everyone in Cutter Gap was wearing their Sunday-best clothes, which for most people here in this community were not much more than rags. Christy's dress was by far the nicest. It was Miss Alice Henderson's birthday, and Christy and David had arranged a party in her honor.

Miss Alice had been a pillar in the community ever since she helped establish the mission school where Christy taught.

She cared for the sick and ministered to the needy. And Miss Alice had often been a wise voice in times of trouble. Everyone from this mountain cove knew and respected her. People had even come from as far away as El Pano and Cataleechie, over rugged mountain trails, to attend her birthday party.

It was turning out to be quite a celebration too. On this early April afternoon, the air was warm and sweetly scented. The Great Smoky Mountains in this remote corner of Tennessee had finally begun to cast off the winter gloom. Children danced and twirled to the music of dulcimer and fiddle. The mountain women wore sprigs of flowers in their hair. Even Cutter Gap's gruff Dr. Neil MacNeill wore a daffodil in his lapel.

It was all so different from the fancy afternoon teas Christy used to attend back home in Asheville, North Carolina. She'd left her well-to-do family to come teach in Cutter Gap just four months ago. When she'd first arrived, these mountain people had seemed backward, poor, and uneducated. Sometimes Christy had even found them frightening. But many things had changed—herself included—in those few short months. And now, when she looked around the lawn, she saw past the shabby clothes and the bare feet. Instead, among the crowd she saw some of her students and her friends. And the memories of Asheville seemed a little dull by comparison.

David had just put his arm around Christy's waist when suddenly three large hogs came racing across the lawn, squealing loudly. They were being chased by Creed Allen, an energetic nine-year-old. Two of the hogs, which lived under the school, had bright pink bows tied around their necks. Creed was carrying a third bow.

Christy and David had to jump back to avoid being

trampled. "'Scuse us, Miz Christy and Preacher," Creed yelled as he ran.

"Looks like Creed is dressing the school pigs for Miss Alice's party," David said.

"I'm certain that Miss Alice will feel honored," Christy said with a laugh. "Now, where were we?"

Again David put his arm around Christy's waist. Awkwardly, Christy placed her hand on David's shoulder. He was taller than she was by several inches, with a lean build and wide-set brown eyes.

"You look quite lovely this afternoon," David said a little nervously. "Like . . . like the prettiest flower in these mountains." He looked at the ground and shrugged. "Sorry. Awfully corny, I know. I guess I speak a better sermon than I do a compliment."

"It was a wonderful compliment," Christy said. "Not that I deserve it, mind you."

And the truth was she didn't. She knew that her face was a little too plain, her blue eyes a little too big, for her to ever be considered truly beautiful. Still, she felt almost beautiful, seeing the way David was looking at her with a mixture of hope and nervousness.

On the front porch of the mission house, several of the mountain men played a sprightly tune. Jeb Spencer, the father of several of Christy's students, was strumming his dulcimer, a boxlike stringed instrument with a sweet tone. Duggin Morrison was tapping a pair of spoons on his knee while Tom McHone sawed away on a worn-looking fiddle.

The doors and the windows of the white, three-story mission house were wide open. From the living room came the sounds of the mission's new grand piano, as Wraight Holt, one of Christy's older students, played along.

Before Christy and David could begin dancing, the song came to an end. "All right, then," David said with a rueful laugh, "we'll dance this next tune."

"How come you're not playing your ukelele, David?" Christy asked.

"There's plenty of time for that," David said. "I wanted to dance with you first. And as soon as Tom gets done tuning that fiddle of his . . ."

Christy laughed. "You may regret it."

"I could never regret it," David said, suddenly sounding very sincere. Then he laughed again. "Besides, you're the one being brave, risking your feet this way."

"Not so brave," came a male voice from nearby. "After all, she danced with me at the mission open house a while back. I doubt you can be any worse a dancer than I, David."

Christy grinned as Dr. MacNeill strode over. He was a big, ruggedly handsome man. His tousled red hair gave him a boyish look. He had a way of smiling at Christy with his hazel eyes that made her feel like he could read her mind.

"Oh, you weren't so bad," Christy teased. The truth was the doctor had turned out to be a surprisingly good dancer, but there was no point in telling David that. She had noticed there were times when the two men seemed to aggravate each other. Christy wasn't sure if it was because they disagreed on many things, like religion. Or if it was—as some had told her—that they both had a romantic interest in Christy.

"I was going to ask you for this dance," the doctor said to Christy. He cast a wry grin at David. "But I can see I'm too late."

"Maybe the next dance," Christy said, feeling her cheeks heat up. "That is, if I survive this one!"

"Well, we'd better make it soon. I hear talk of a horse race starting soon over in the field," the doctor cautioned.

"Once that gets started, we'll lose our musicians, I wager. They'll all be wanting to watch."

"Sorry, Doc," David said, with a tiny hint of a smug smile. "Better luck next time."

"The lady's got a mind of her own," the doctor warned. "Watch yourself or she'll try to lead!"

The music started up again, a jaunty tune led by Tom McHone's fiddle. David swung Christy around and they started across the yard. It was still a bit muddy, but fresh bright-green grass was making an appearance, cushioning the mostly bare feet of the dancers.

They had only gone a few steps when a hand tapped on David's right shoulder. He stopped and spun around. "Don't tell me you're trying to cut in, Dr.—" he began.

But it wasn't the doctor. Ruby Mae Morrison, a red-haired, freckled thirteen-year-old, was standing behind him. "Miz Christy," she said breathlessly, "you just got to help me!"

"What's wrong, Ruby Mae?" Christy asked, speaking loudly to be heard over the music.

"And can't it wait?" David asked impatiently. "The dance is already half over. And I was finally getting the hang of that step—"

Ruby Mae shook her head regretfully. "Truth to tell, Preacher," she said, "you weren't even close. When the good Lord was passin' out feet, he musta given you two left ones."

"Don't listen to her, David," Christy said. "I still have all the feeling in most of my toes. Now, what is it, Ruby Mae?"

"I was wantin' to ask you private-like first . . ." Ruby Mae hesitated.

"Whatever you have to say, you can say to Mr. Grantland too."

Ruby Mae twirled a finger around a long lock of hair. "Actually, it do sort of involve Preacher. It's just that I was a-hopin' you could . . . Well, my mama always says you can get a man to take the bitterest medicine if'n you sweeten it first with honey."

David crossed his arms over his chest. "Come on, Ruby Mae. Miss Christy's not going to sweeten me up. I can't be sweetened."

"Oh, is that right?" Christy asked, fluttering her eyelashes at David.

David ignored her. "Out with it," he said to Ruby Mae.

Ruby Mae took a deep breath, then let the words tumble out. "I want to race Prince 'cause I just know I can beat the pants off'n the rest of the men 'cause you know he's plumb faster than the wind when I'm a-ridin' him. But I can't less'n you say so 'cause he belongs to the mission and please, please, please say it's all right, Preacher."

She took another deep breath, smiled wide, and batted her eyes. "So I reckon the answer's yes?"

David shook his head. "Assuming I understood you correctly, I'm afraid the answer's no." He patted her on the shoulder. "Too bad they're not having a talking race. You'd be sure to win, Ruby Mae."

Ruby Mae groaned. "But, Preacher—"

"No buts, Ruby Mae."

"But wouldn't you just burst with pride if'n Prince won?

Everybody in Cutter Gap would be a-sayin, 'That preacher owns the finest horse in these here mountains!'"

"To begin with, I don't own Prince. He belongs to the mission."

"You may as well own him," Ruby Mae said. "Everybody thinks of him as your horse. You're always ridin' Prince here and there when you minister to folks, sittin' proud and lookin' all fine and fancy."

"The answer is still no, Ruby Mae."

"But why?" she persisted, turning her pleading gaze on Christy.

"Are you sure she can't, David?" Christy asked. "After all, Ruby Mae's been riding Prince every day since he was donated to the mission. And she is a wonderful rider."

Ruby Mae tugged on David's arm. "Miz Christy's right," she said.

David gave Christy a skeptical look. "What Miss Christy doesn't realize is that when the mountain people throw a race, the prize is usually a bottle of illegal liquor."

"Moonshine?" Christy cried.

Just then, the music came to a stop and the dancers parted, panting and laughing.

"Now look." David pouted. "We missed our dance."

"Next time," Christy promised. "Now, Ruby Mae, tell me the truth—is David right? Is this a race for moonshine?"

"I don't care none about the prize," Ruby Mae said. "It ain't about that."

"I think maybe David's right, Ruby Mae. Besides, it might be dangerous."

"Ain't dangerous," Ruby Mae said. "Just flat-out racin' in

the field over yonder. No jumpin' or turnin', Miz Christy. Easy as pie."

"Still, it's Mr. Grantland's decision. He's the one who takes care of Prince."

"But like you say, Prince is the mission's horse," Ruby Mae argued. "And besides, I'm the one what's been muckin' out his stall and givin' him baths and kissin' him goodnight."

David grinned. "She has a point. I never kiss Prince goodnight."

"And it is true she's been spending a lot of time with Prince," Christy added. She rolled her eyes. "Some might even say too much time, judging from the way she's been shirking some of her chores and schoolwork."

"I promise I'll do better on my chores and homework, Miz Christy," Ruby Mae said. "But you just gotta let me race. For all us gal-women in the Cove."

"What do you mean?" Christy asked.

"I mean none of them smarty-pants men thinks a girl can win."

One of the musicians nearby laughed loudly. Christy looked over to see Duggin Morrison, Ruby Mae's stepfather, spit out a brown stream of tobacco. With his long white beard and wrinkled skin, he looked old enough to be her grandfather. Ruby Mae and her stepfather had been having trouble getting along, so she was staying at the mission house with Christy and David's sister, Miss Ida.

"No gal-woman can beat the Taylors' horse, Lightning," Duggin said. "'Specially no spoiled-rotten, trouble-makin', no-good stepdaughter o' mine."

"Hush up, Daddy," Ruby Mae said. "I can so ride better than any man in Cutter Gap."

"You hear how she sasses me?" Duggin cried. "Talkin' like that to her own step-pa!"

Christy pulled Ruby Mae away from Duggin. There was no point in starting up a family feud right in the middle of Miss Alice's party.

Christy and David led Ruby Mae over to the schoolhouse, which also served as the church on Sundays. Miss Alice was sitting on the porch steps, calmly watching the festivities with her gentle deep-gray gaze. She was wearing a long green dress, and her slightly graying hair was swept up in a bun. Her right arm sat in a sling. She'd sprained her wrist last week when she'd slipped on a muddy incline on her way to help deliver a baby in a remote cabin.

"What do you think about Ruby Mae riding in the race?" Christy asked.

"Well, she's a fine rider, no doubt about that," Miss Alice said. "And Prince has incredible speed. Not like my Goldie," she said fondly. Miss Alice's sturdy palomino was getting on in years.

"Oh, Prince do have speed, Miss Alice, he do," Ruby Mae cried. "One day last week I ran him straight over Big Spoon Creek, and he jumped so high I thought I'd touch heaven—" She glanced over at David, who was frowning. "Oops. Don't get me wrong. It were just a little jump, Preacher, I promise."

Dr. MacNeill joined them. He was eating one of the gingerbread cookies that Fairlight Spencer had brought for the celebration. "I watched you two dancing," said the doctor with a grin. "That was some fancy footwork, David. All ten seconds' worth."

"We were interrupted," David grumbled.

"Probably a good thing," the doctor joked. "How's that wrist of yours, Miss Alice?"

"Still swollen," Miss Alice said. "But I'll be fine soon. Wish it had been my left hand. I can't even write my name. And it makes my nursing duties difficult."

Ruby Mae tugged on David's sleeve. "You heard Miss Alice, Preacher. Can I ride Prince?"

"Not if there's moonshine involved," David said firmly.

"I hate to think there's illegal liquor here at your birthday party," Christy said to Miss Alice.

"Oh, it's here, whether we like it or not," said the doctor. "Moonshine's a part of mountain life."

"I'm afraid the doctor's right," Miss Alice said. "Bird's-Eye Taylor appears to have consumed quite a bit already." She nodded over toward the lattice-covered springhouse where Bird's-Eye was dozing, snoring loudly. His dirty felt hat covered one eye.

Christy shook her head. Bird's-Eye was the father of her most difficult and troublesome student, seventeen-year-old Lundy. Lundy was big and mean, a constant bully with a chip on his shoulder. From what Christy had seen of his father, it was easy to see why Lundy was so difficult.

"So is the answer no?" Ruby Mae pressed again. "Or yes?"

"I can't let you ride in a race for moonshine," David said. "As a matter of fact, I won't let a race like that take place here at all."

"I've already taken care of that," Miss Alice said with a grin. "I put up two of Miss Ida's apple pies as a prize for the winner of the race, instead of liquor. As much as liquor is prized in this Cove, Miss Ida's pies are even more coveted."

David laughed. "My sister does make a fine pie."

"For my part, David, I think you should let Ruby Mae enter the race," Miss Alice said. "She has as good a chance as any of the men."

"And it would teach them a lesson," Christy added. "Sometimes I'm amazed at the way men treat women here in Cutter Gap."

"Miz Christy is right," Ruby Mae said. "These men got no respect for womenfolks."

"I don't know," David said, rubbing his chin.

Just then, Ruby Mae's stepfather sauntered by. He was weaving a little, as if he might have been drinking too. "Don't you bother racin', gal," he yelled. "You ain't got a chance, Ruby Mae."

Christy spun around. "Mr. Morrison, I think you're going to have to eat your words. Ruby Mae on Prince can beat any man."

David rolled his eyes. "I didn't give permission yet," he reminded her.

"But you were going to, weren't you?" Christy asked, giving him a nudge.

David shook his head and sighed. "I can tell when I'm outnumbered. Come on, Ruby Mae. I'll help you get Prince saddled up."

# Two

Ruby Mae stood next to Prince, stroking his glossy neck. They were waiting by the starting line for all the other riders and their horses. "You and me, boy," she whispered to the beautiful black stallion. "We're a-goin' to show them others."

"Don't count on it." Lundy Taylor strode up on Lightning. The big gray stallion gave a hard nudge on Prince's shoulder.

Ruby Mae rolled her eyes. It figured. Even the Taylors' horse was mean. Meanness just plain ran in the family. Maybe it was because Bird's-Eye, Lundy's pa, was a moonshiner. Of course, Ruby Mae's own step-pa had done his share of moon-shinin' too.

"You ain't got a chance, Ruby Mae Morrison," Lundy said with a sneer. "Womenfolk is good for two things: cookin' and jabberin'. Lord knows you know how to talk. I don't know what kind of cook you is, but one way or t'other, you ain't got a chance, you and that preacher-horse."

"Just you wait and see, Lundy," Ruby Mae shot back. She

ran her hand through Prince's mane, soft and long as the silk in an ear of corn. "Prince is faster'n a fox on fire. You'll see."

She gazed around at the other entrants. Jake Pentland—nephew of Ben Pentland, the local mailman—was there with a stocky little chestnut mare. Elias Tuttle—the owner of the general store in El Pano, a town about seven miles from Cutter Gap—was riding up on a fancy bay gelding with a wonderful leather saddle, all shiny and tooled. Elias often donated food and supplies to Miz Alice for the mission.

Just then someone rode up on the other side of her. It was Rob Allen, a tall, slender fourteen-year-old who was one of the best students at school. Miz Christy had even appointed him a Junior Teacher who got to help the other students. Rob was riding a piebald mare named Pegasus, a name Rob had gotten from one of the books he liked to read. Of course "Pegasus" was such a mouthful that most folks just called the horse "Peg."

Rob wanted to be a writer when he grew up. Ruby Mae thought that was a grand idea. She wished she wanted to be something, too, but she hadn't quite figured out what she hoped for. She knew she wished her hair wouldn't act like it had a mind of its own on humid summer afternoons. She knew she wished her freckles weren't so darn . . . well, freckle-y. And she knew she wished she had two whole pairs of leather shoes as fine and fancy as Miz Christy's.

But those things didn't nearly seem as good as wanting to be something bigger than all outdoors, like a writer. Ruby Mae thought Rob was very special for wanting something so huge and impossible and fine. She also thought he had the cutest little bitty dimple in his cheek when he smiled just so, but of course she'd never told him that. And he looked mighty tall, sitting astride his horse and gazing down at her.

"You going to race Peg?" Ruby Mae asked Rob.

"Why, Pegasus is plumb fast when she puts her mind to it." Rob smiled shyly. "'Course, she's got a mind of her own. Never do know when she's in the mood to run."

"I s'pose you're goin' to tell me how I ain't got a chance of winnin'," Ruby Mae said.

"Nope. I seen you ridin' Prince. For a girl, you handle a horse fine. Even for a man, I reckon." He gave a cockeyed grin, then shrugged. "Truth is you ride like you was part horse yourself, Ruby Mae."

Ruby Mae could hardly keep from hollering, she was so thrilled at Rob's words. No man or boy had ever admitted to her before that she was a good rider. But all she said was, "Well, then, may the best man . . . or gal . . . win."

By now, quite a crowd had formed to watch the race. Everywhere Ruby Mae looked, it seemed like she saw happy couples. It must be because spring was in the air. Lizette Holcombe was holding hands with Wraight Holt, who'd stopped playing the piano to come watch the fun. Bessie Coburn, Ruby Mae's best friend, was whispering to John Spencer, a boy Bessie'd had a crush on for what seemed like forever and a day. And as for Miz Christy—well, she seemed to have two fellows sweet on her: the doctor and the preacher. Miz Christy said Ruby Mae was imagining things, but Ruby Mae had an eye for romance. She could tell the doctor and the preacher both liked Miz Christy all right. Question was which one was Miz Christy hankering after?

Of course, Ruby Mae was in love too—but not with any fellow. She was in love with a horse. Since Prince had come to the mission, it was all she could do to think about anything else. Before school, after school, sometimes during school, if she could find an excuse. Ruby Mae spent every waking moment thinking about Prince. She'd always loved animals, from the little three-footed squirrel she'd nursed back to health after he'd been attacked by an animal to the old owl who lived in the sycamore near her cabin. But Prince was different. When she was riding him, she felt like anything was possible.

"Ruby Mae, you be careful, now, ya hear?"

Ruby Mae looked over to see her mother approaching. Her graying hair was tied with a piece of frayed rope. In the bright sunshine, the harsh lines in her face made her look even more worn and tired than usual.

"I will, Ma," Ruby Mae promised. She toyed with her reins. "I . . . I miss you and Pa."

"You can come visit any time. Ain't like you don't know the way." Mrs. Morrison nodded at Prince. "Looks like you're gettin' spoiled, livin' here with that teacher in the mission house. Your own horse to ride, plenty of food . . ." She clucked her tongue at Ruby Mae's braids, the ones Miz Christy had taught her to make. "Why, I'll just bet you take a bath in that metal tub of theirs every single day."

Ruby Mae hesitated. She didn't know what to say. The truth was she did like living at the mission house. She missed her parents, but they were always yelling at each other and at her. It was a relief to get away from all the fussing. When Miss Alice had first suggested that Ruby Mae stay at the mission house for a while, Ruby Mae had wondered if it was a good idea. But now she knew that it was.

"Maybe I can come back home soon, Ma," Ruby Mae said

softly. She wondered if Rob was listening. She glanced over at him, but he was fiddling with his stirrups. Ruby Mae lowered her voice. "But it just seems like whenever we're all together, we start in on fightin' like wildcats in a flour sack."

"If you weren't so ornery," Mrs. Morrison began, "that mouth of yours runnin' on like a waterfall—" She stopped. "Well, no point in startin' that again. I just wanted to say be careful, is all."

From behind them came a drunken whoop. It was Bird's-Eye, Lundy's father, with Ruby Mae's stepfather. Bird's-Eye was walking lopsidedly, leaning on Duggin for support.

"Looky here!" Bird's-Eye cried. "That your stepdaughter, Duggin? She think she's a boy, do she?"

"Told her she ain't got a prayer of winnin', but you know that Ruby Mae," Duggin said, propping up Bird's-Eye as he nearly tripped. "That gal gets a notion in her head, it's stuck there like honey in a hive."

Mrs. Morrison scowled. "Don't pay him no nevermind, girl," she whispered. "I seen you ride before. You can beat 'em all, if'n you put that stubborn will of your'n to it."

"Yes, ma'am," Ruby Mae said. She smiled gratefully at her mother, then put her left foot in the stirrup and swung herself up onto Prince's sleek back. She nudged him gently toward the starting line. She was proud of the way he stood there, ready to run but calm. Not fidgeting and fussing like some of the other horses.

Miss Alice appeared in front of the line of riders. She winked at Ruby Mae, and Ruby Mae gave her a thumbs-up to show she was confident. Ruby Mae loved Miss Alice. Miss Alice had a way of talking about God that made Him seem not so fearsome and far away, but kind and loving and close as your own heartbeat.

"All right, I see we have our riders assembled," Miss Alice said. "Lundy Taylor on Lightning. Jake Pentland on Robert E. Lee. Elias Tuttle on Possum. Ruby Mae Morrison on Prince—"

At the sound of Ruby Mae's name, Duggin and Bird's-Eye, along with some of the other men, began to hoot and whistle.

Rob looked over at her and winked. "Don't pay 'em no nevermind," he said.

"And last but not least," Miss Alice continued, "Rob Allen on Pegasus. Now, as this is my birthday, I will officiate over the race, to be sure it's run fair and square. On the count of three, you will race to the edge of the field to that big oak, turn, and come back to this spot. Be careful on that turn, by the way. It's a tight one. Winner receives two of Miss Ida's finest apple pies."

"Woulda liked a jug o' likker better," Lundy grumbled.

Miss Alice ignored him. "Are there any questions?"

"Can't rightly start a race without a gun," said Ruby Mae's stepfather. He waved his shotgun in the air. "Ain't proper."

"There'll be no shooting at my birthday party, Duggin Morrison," Miss Alice warned. She spoke so quietly and firmly that he put down his gun. Miss Alice had a way about her, Ruby Mae thought, smiling to herself. She could put the fear of God into any man, even Ruby Mae's stepfather.

"But on second thought, Duggin," Miss Alice continued with a smile, "since my own hand is temporarily out of order, I'll allow you to start the riders off, on the count of three. One shot straight up, Duggin, and that's all, understood?"

Ruby Mae's stepfather grinned. He pointed his old hunting rifle toward the sky.

"Riders, are you ready?" Miss Alice called.

Everyone nodded. "Ready to beat the pants off'n the rest o' these losers!" Lundy cried.

Ruby Mae cast a quick smile at Rob. She bent down and whispered to Prince, "We can beat 'em all, boy. You just show 'em what you're made of, and so will I." She looked back and saw Miz Christy watching her. Miz Christy held up her fingers, to show they were crossed for good luck.

"On your marks," Miss Alice called. A hush fell over the crowd.

"Get set," she said.

Ruby crouched low, tightening her grip on the reins. She could feel Prince tense beneath her. His ears were pricked. He pounded a foot on the ground.

He was ready, and so was Ruby Mae.

Duggin Morrison fired his gun. The powerful blast shook the air.

"Hah, boy!" Ruby Mae pressed her bare heels into Prince's sides and gave him plenty of rein as he thrust into a full gallop. To her left, Lundy's horse, Lightning, and Elias' horse, Possum, were neck and neck, just a few yards ahead of her. To her right, Peg and Robert E. Lee had fallen back.

"Atta boy!" she screamed. Prince's hooves slashed the grass, filling the air with a noise like slow thunder. He was flying, that was all there was to it. If she didn't know better, she'd swear the mighty horse had wings.

Ruby Mae kept her eyes focused on the great oak at the end of the field. It would be a tricky turn. She'd have to slow Prince down enough to take it sharply and avoid running into the other riders. But she didn't want to slow down too much. Especially not when Prince was starting to overtake Lightning and Possum.

Down the field they flew. She could hear the whooping and hollering of the crowd behind her. But this was no time to think about them. She needed to think about Prince.

By the time she reached the tree, Ruby Mae and Lundy were in the lead as their two stallions, Lightning and Prince, struggled to win. She eased to the right of the tree, while Lundy and his horse went to the left. It was all she could do to rein in Prince. The leather straps burned in her hands as she slowed him down to a fast trot. "Whoa, boy, whoa," she cried. "We're only halfway home."

At the sound of her voice, Prince responded instantly. Pulling hard on the left rein, Ruby Mae turned him in a tight veer. She nearly lost her balance, the turn was so sharp, but she grabbed a hunk of Prince's mane and held on for dear life.

She was still trying to regain her seat as she signaled him back into an all-out gallop. Possum, Robert E. Lee, and Peg were just approaching the tree. The field ahead of her was clear. She didn't want to look around for Lundy and lose a precious second.

"Go, Prince!" Ruby Mae cried, giving him a hard kick with her heels.

Just then, she heard the sound of thundering hooves coming from her right. It was Lightning, closing in fast. He was going to ram right into her!

"I'll get you yet, preacher horse!" Lundy screamed.

Frantically, Ruby Mae yanked back on the reins. Prince hesitated, then pulled back to a trot. Lundy and Lightning zoomed past, just inches from Prince's head.

*What if I hadn't slowed?* Ruby Mae wondered for a split second. Was Lundy such a bully that he would have risked his own horse? Or was he just sure that, because she was a girl, she would stop to save Prince . . . and herself?

*Well,* she thought fiercely, *there's no point in being too sure, Lundy Taylor.*

"Get him, Prince!" Ruby Mae screamed. She pushed him into a full gallop, and Prince was glad for the chance.

Twenty yards ahead of them—an impossible distance to make up—Lundy and Lightning were flying across the field to the cheers of the crowd. *We don't have a chance,* Ruby Mae thought. She knew there was no way Prince could catch Lightning now.

Fortunately, Prince did not know any such thing. Driven by the sight of another horse so close at hand, he dug his hooves deeper into the soft soil. His neck lunged. His mouth foamed. His feet flew so fast it seemed to Ruby Mae that she and Prince were no longer touching ground at all. Faster and faster, he hurled himself on.

Lundy glanced back. Ruby Mae could see both surprise and panic on his face. He whipped Lightning's shoulder with his reins. "Git on, you old nag!" he screamed.

But it was too late. Prince was not about to let Lightning win. In a final, wild surge, he flung himself forward, past Lundy and the crowd, past Miss Alice, and over the finish line. He didn't want to stop running, didn't seem to care where he was going, as long as he and Ruby Mae could fly through the air together.

Ruby Mae let him circle the crowd, still galloping. Finally she reined him into a fine trot. He pranced across the field toward the cheers, proud and haughty. His head was high, and so was Ruby Mae's. She caught sight of Miz Christy, waving and cheering. Ruby Mae's mother was smiling, nodding her head. Rob Allen, who'd crossed the finish line behind her and Lundy, gave her a wink. Lundy was scowling, of course, shooting daggers at Ruby Mae with his eyes.

Then she noticed her stepfather. His gun was cradled in his arms. He wasn't exactly smiling; you couldn't say that. But he was looking at her like he'd never quite seen her before.

Ruby Mae took one more circle around the field. In spite of Miss Alice's warning, someone shot off a gun in celebration. More shots followed. The cheers and shouts were music in the air. She slowed Prince down to a walk, leaning down long enough to stroke his damp, hot coat.

"Hear those shouts and them guns a-firin', boy?" she crooned. "That's for you. All for you."

Suddenly the shouts and shots silenced. Someone screamed, and then the field grew still.

It wasn't until Ruby Mae rode closer that she saw the fallen figure of Dr. MacNeill lying on the ground in a pool of blood. And nearby stood her stepfather, smoke still spiraling from the barrel of his gun.

# Three

EVEN BEFORE SHE KNEW WHO'D BEEN SHOT, CHRISTY SAW the bright red pool of blood.

Then she heard a child scream. "The doc! The doc's been shot!"

Frantically, Christy pushed her way through the crowd. Dr. MacNeill lay on the ground. He was bleeding badly from his left shoulder. Miss Alice was kneeling next to him. The crowd, murmuring, formed a tight circle around them.

"Neil!" Christy cried. She knelt on the other side of him.

He tried to sit up, but Miss Alice eased him back down. "It's nothing," the doctor said, but his face was pale.

"Why don't you let me be the judge of that?" Miss Alice said as she pressed a handkerchief against the wound with her left hand.

Christy watched, horrified, as the white handkerchief turned deep red.

"You're going to be fine," she assured the doctor, but her voice was shaking. Miss Alice stood up. She seemed to be trying to remove her own sprained right arm from the sling that held it. Christy saw her wince in pain from the attempt. Her eyes, always so calm, were worried. "Let's get you over to the mission house."

Ruby Mae rushed over on Prince. "I'll ride him over, Miss Alice," she said. "If'n he can get a leg up."

"I can walk, thank you all very much," the doctor said. Using Christy for support, he managed to stand with his arm around her shoulder. David rushed to his other side.

"I want to make this perfectly clear," Miss Alice said to the crowd sternly. "I'm going to assume that shot was an accident." She leveled her gaze at Duggin Morrison, who stared down at the ground. "But it was an accident born of mixing moonshine and guns. And those are two things I will not tolerate here at the mission. Next gun I hear go off, next jug of illegal liquor I see poured, I'll be getting my own gun. And you know I'm a better shot than most of you men. Even without the use of my good hand."

Christy and David helped Dr. MacNeill walk a few feet. The doctor's face was white, and his forehead dotted with sweat. Ruby Mae followed closely on Prince.

"Ruby Mae," the doctor said, "I think I may just take you up on that offer after all. By the way," he added with a wink and a weak smile, "that was a fine race."

Ruby Mae slid from the saddle, and with David's help, the doctor climbed onto Prince. "I feel so bad about this, Doctor," Ruby Mae muttered as she led Prince toward the mission house with Christy, David, and Miss Alice close at hand. "It were my step-pa what shot you, I 'spect," she muttered. "Dang drunk that he is."

"It could have been anyone, Ruby Mae," the doctor assured her. "Everyone was shooting off their guns."

"No, it was him," Ruby Mae muttered. "I heard him tell Ma that he was shooting toward the clouds, but he lost his balance and the gun went off."

"I'll tell you what to blame," David muttered angrily. "Blame the liquor in those jugs. Blame the moonshine these mountain people insist on making and drinking and selling."

"That's something you can't hope to change, David," said the doctor wearily. "Take it from me. I've lived in these mountains a long time. You're new here."

"It's something I'm going to change, you just wait and see," David said firmly.

"There's plenty of time for this talk later," Miss Alice interrupted as they approached the steps of the mission house. "Let's get the doctor inside."

David helped Dr. MacNeill climb down off Prince. The doctor groaned on landing, then reluctantly leaned on David for support.

"Ruby Mae," Miss Alice directed, "run on over to my cabin and fetch my medical bag, will you?"

In the upstairs hallway, Miss Alice pulled Christy aside while David helped the doctor into bed.

"I'm going to need you to help get that bullet out of the doctor," Miss Alice whispered. "Without my right hand, I'm not much of a surgeon."

"Me?" Christy cried in horror. "Help with . . . But I don't know the first thing about surgery—"

"How about during your journey here, when the doctor had to do that operation on Bob Allen? You helped him then, didn't you?" Miss Alice patted her on the arm. "That makes you more experienced than either David or Ruby Mae. And they're the only other two possibilities."

"But I can't—"

"Don't worry, dear. I'll help you through it. And the Lord will guide your hands."

Reluctantly, Christy followed Miss Alice into the bedroom. At the sight of the broadening stain across the doctor's shirt, her stomach did a sharp somersault. Somewhere beneath that shirt was a bullet—a bullet that Miss Alice expected her to remove. She felt her knees buckle under her, and she reached for a chair.

"Better keep an eye on that girl," the doctor joked. "She's turning the nicest shade of green you ever did see."

"I'm fine," Christy said through clenched teeth.

"What would you call that, Preacher?" the doctor continued, determined to seem unconcerned. "Spring green? Or maybe it's more of an emerald green—"

"I'm fine," Christy repeated more firmly.

Miss Alice helped the doctor remove his shirt. His broad chest was smeared with blood. Carefully she felt the area of the wound.

"Watch your poking," the doctor muttered, wincing.

He felt the wound himself, grimacing as his fingers ran over the bullet. "Not so deep at all," he pronounced. "No fractures. A little messy, but no problem to remove."

Ruby Mae clumped up the stairs and rushed into the bedroom, carrying Miss Alice's bag. Following close behind was Miss Ida, David's prudish and fussy older sister.

"Oh my goodness!" Ida cried. "I was just putting the finishing touches on Miss Alice's cake when I heard the ruckus up here. What on earth happened? Look at this mess!"

"Moonshine and guns," David said darkly. "They don't mix."

"You can just bring that bag to me, Ruby Mae," the doctor instructed. She set it next to him, and he began digging through its contents.

"Miss Ida, we could use some boiling water and fresh towels," Miss Alice said.

"Of course," Miss Ida said. "Will he be all right?"

"I expect so. The doctor's pretty tough," Miss Alice said with a forced smile.

The doctor removed a scalpel and a pair of forceps from Miss Alice's bag. "Just what exactly is it you're preparing to do, Neil?" Miss Alice asked.

"I'm going to remove the bullet, of course," he said.

"Lordamercy!" Ruby Mae cried. "He's the bravest man what ever lived, I reckon!"

"There's a fine line between bravery and foolishness, Ruby Mae," said Miss Alice. Turning to the doctor, she said curtly, "As I recall, you're left-handed, are you not, Neil?"

"That I am." He dug through her bag, muttering to himself. "Where do you keep your needles and suturing thread, anyway?"

"And," Miss Alice continued, pulling the bag away from him, "isn't that bullet in your left shoulder?"

Doctor MacNeill looked up at Miss Alice. His expression was a mixture of pain, amusement, and annoyance. "I see what you're getting at, Miss Alice. But you and I are the only medical practitioners for a hundred miles or more, and, nothing personal, but I'd rather go at this bullet myself than have you try to remove it with that sprained hand of yours." He gave her a wry look. "As I recall, you're right-handed, are you not? And isn't that your right hand in a sling?" He sat up a little straighter, wincing at the pain. "So it looks like I'm elected."

Miss Alice shook her head. "Christy will do the surgery."

"Christy!" the doctor cried. "Not likely! Just look at her! She's the color of a green apple! And you expect me to let her pull a bullet out of my own flesh?"

"We have no choice," Miss Alice said.

"Believe me, I would rather not have to play doctor," Christy said. "But—"

"You! You'd rather not? How do you think I feel about it?" the doctor cried. "You're a teacher, not a doctor."

"Lordamercy," Ruby Mae said in a loud whisper, "this is even more excitin' than the race!"

"Behave, Neil," Miss Alice chided. "You're acting like a child. You and I both know there's often not much more to surgery than being a good tailor."

The doctor grabbed Miss Alice's hand. "Please," he said. "Have mercy. I beg of you. I've heard about Christy's seamstress efforts. Granny O'Teale said her quilting skills leave a lot to be desired."

"I'm a fine seamstress!" Christy cried indignantly.

"Actually, Miz Christy," Ruby Mae interjected, "those buttons you done sewed on Mountie O'Teale's coat a while back fell off. Remember how you had to stitch 'em all on again?"

"Oh, wonderful." The doctor covered his eyes with his right hand, groaning.

Miss Ida reappeared with a pile of towels. She had torn them into strips to use for bandages. "The water's boiling," she announced.

"Good," Christy said, taking the towels. "Let's get these

instruments sterilized so we can get this over with." She looked at Miss Alice. "Right?"

"Exactly," Miss Alice said.

Miss Ida gasped. She gazed at Miss Alice's arm in its sling, then at the doctor's wound. "Oh, my," she whispered. "What is the world coming to when Christy Huddleston is our only medical hope?"

"Thank you for that vote of confidence, Miss Ida," Christy said with a sigh.

Miss Ida patted the doctor's forearm gently.

When everything was ready at last, Christy washed her hands thoroughly in a basin, then positioned herself in a chair beside the doctor's bed. Miss Alice stood behind her, observing and instructing. David and Ruby Mae watched from a distance.

"First, you'll need to cleanse the area of the wound," Miss Alice instructed.

Christy bit her lip. Her stomach felt queasy. Her hands were shaking.

She met the doctor's eyes. He was smiling at her weakly, looking at her with that way he had when she was certain he was reading her mind.

"You'll do fine," the doctor said gently.

Christy took a deep, steadying breath. "I hope so."

"You did fine when you helped me with Bob Allen," the doctor reminded her. "You're stronger than you think, Christy Huddleston. I only hope I am too."

Christy cast him a grateful smile. "I'll do my best."

When Christy had cleaned the wound, Miss Alice leaned close to examine it. "You're going to need to make a small incision to reach the slug," she said. "Pick up the scalpel."

Christy picked up the sharp blade. She forced her hand to stop trembling.

"Hold the scalpel firmly in your right hand while you feel the position of the bullet with your left," Miss Alice instructed. "Then draw a small line, maybe a half an inch from the point of entry, with the scalpel. Press firmly."

"But not too firmly," the doctor added with a reassuring smile.

Christy closed her eyes. *Please, Lord*, she prayed silently, *give me the strength to meet this challenge.*

"It helps," the doctor suggested, "if you open your eyes."

"I was praying for assistance," Christy explained.

"Wonderful," the doctor moaned.

Steadying her shaking hands, Christy did as Miss Alice instructed. Suddenly the joking mood vanished. Everyone was silent. She could feel the doctor go rigid as she pressed the scalpel down.

"Fine, fine," Miss Alice said.

Christy lifted the scalpel and looked over at the doctor. His eyes were closed, the muscles of his handsome face tight as he grimaced against the pain.

"This ain't turnin' out nearly like I thought," Ruby Mae whispered, rushing from the room.

"I'll go see if Ruby Mae's all right," David offered quickly.

As David darted toward the door, Christy noticed that he looked a little green himself.

"Now, wipe away that blood," Miss Alice said.

Christy did as she was instructed. To her relief, the queasiness had passed. Now she just wanted to finish the operation as quickly as possible to spare the doctor any more pain.

"Take that small pair of forceps and, using your other

hand, locate the bullet. You may need to poke around a little." Miss Alice placed a cool cloth over the doctor's forehead. "You doing all right, Neil? I would offer you some ether, but I know you'd never take it."

"Oh, no," he said through gritted teeth. "Go to sleep while Christy is carving me like a Thanksgiving turkey? Not likely."

Carefully, Christy eased the forceps closer to the bullet. With each fraction of an inch, she could feel the doctor's pain as if it were her own. Once he groaned out loud.

"I'm hurting you," Christy wailed desperately.

"No," the doctor said. "Keep going. You're almost there. You're doing fine."

Christy searched Miss Alice's face. "I can't do this, Miss Alice."

"Of course you can," she encouraged.

Again Christy struggled to find the bullet. Once she managed to get the ends around the slug, but when she tried to pull, the forceps came free. She did not let herself look at the doctor's face. She couldn't bear it. But she could see his chest rising and falling quickly, and she could see his fists balled tightly.

"I can't seem to reach it," Christy said after another unsuccessful try.

"Yes, you can," the doctor said. She could hear the pain in his voice. "You can do anything you set your mind to, Christy."

Again Christy tried. This time, when she reached the bullet, she tightened her grip on the forceps and held tight to the bullet. It came free at last. She stared at the big twisted piece of bloody lead. Her fingers were trembling again. Just a few inches more and it might have struck the doctor's heart. This bullet was a symbol of all that was wrong and dangerous and evil in these beautiful mountains.

She let the slug drop into a basin.

"Fine job," Miss Alice said, squeezing Christy's shoulders.

"Not bad for a first-timer," the doctor said weakly.

Christy let herself meet his eyes. She saw terrible pain there, but a half smile still waited for her. He touched her arm with his hand. "I knew you could do it."

"Now, let's get that incision sutured up," Miss Alice said.

The doctor sighed. "Was that really true about Mountie's buttons?"

Christy smiled. "Yes," she admitted. "But I've been taking quilting lessons from some local women since then. I've improved, really I have."

"Oh, well," the doctor said with another sigh. "At least it will make an interesting scar."

## *Four*

"HOW ARE YOU FEELING?" CHRISTY ASKED THE NEXT MORN-
ing as she carried a breakfast tray into the doctor's room.

"Like someone shot me in the shoulder." The doctor sat
up slowly, groaning. His hair was mussed, and there were
dark circles under his eyes. A fresh white bandage covered
much of his shoulder. His arm sat in a sling.

"You look terrible," Christy said, placing the tray on his
lap. She plumped his pillows.

"Talk to my surgeon. She's the one responsible," the doctor said as he took a sip of coffee.

"Actually, Miss Alice told me she already examined your
stitches this morning, and she said they looked beautiful."

"Well, they're holding so far, which is more than we can
say for Mountie O'Teale's buttons," the doctor teased. He
lifted the napkin covering a bowl of oatmeal and frowned.
"What exactly is this?" he demanded.

"Miss Ida made you oatmeal. Ruby Mae helped. She put a
little molasses and cinnamon in it for flavor."

The doctor took one bite then rolled his eyes. He set the

tray aside. "I think it's time for me to be heading on home where I can make my own breakfast. Something that doesn't involve Ruby Mae's special flavor."

"You'll do no such thing," Christy said firmly, pushing him back against the pillow.

He winced. "Watch it. Your bedside manner needs a little work."

"Sorry," Christy apologized. "But Miss Alice said you've got a low fever. You need to stay here until we're sure you're healing properly."

"Yes, Doctor," he grumbled to Christy.

"I'm just quoting Miss Alice," Christy said defensively. She handed him the tray again, and he took it reluctantly. "She also told me that doctors make terrible patients."

"She's right about that, I'll wager."

Christy put her fingers on the doctor's forehead. "You do feel a little warm."

He reached up and held her hand. His own was large and strong and warm to the touch.

"I want to thank you for what you did yesterday," he said. "I know how hard it was for you. And despite my teasing, I knew you would do a first-rate job. And that you did." Then he added with a chuckle, "Far better than I would have done, trying to stand in as a teacher to that huge class of rambunctious children you teach."

"Thank you for saying that," Christy said, suddenly feeling shy under his intense gaze.

Just then, David knocked on the door and peered inside. At the sight of Christy and the doctor holding hands, he stammered, "Maybe . . . Should I come back?"

"No, come on in, David," Christy said quickly, withdrawing her hand.

David cleared his throat. "So how's the patient?" he asked. He was dressed in his proper ministerial clothes—striped pants, a white shirt, and a dark tie. His hair was carefully combed. Christy always thought he looked older and more dignified on Sundays.

"The patient is already complaining," Christy said. "I'm not sure if that's a good sign or not."

"I happen to be suffering in silence." The doctor held up his coffee cup. "You know, Christy, as much pain as you put me through, I could really use something stronger. A little of that moonshine would come in handy right around now."

"How can you joke about that?" Christy cried. "It's moonshine that nearly got you killed! What if that bullet had been a few inches nearer your heart? What if Duggin had hit your head?" She rolled her eyes. "Come to think of it, if he'd hit your head, the bullet would probably just have ricocheted off."

David nodded. "I agree with Christy, Doctor. As a matter of fact, my sermon this morning is going to be on the evils of moonshine. I'm hoping it will have some effect."

"Take my advice, David." The doctor poked at his oatmeal with a spoon. "Don't go meddling where you don't belong."

"Meddling?" David demanded. "You're sitting there with a hole in you, talking about meddling? Maybe you think these mountain men can guzzle all the homemade liquor they please, but when they endanger others . . . Suppose that bullet had hit a child, Doctor? What then?"

The doctor leveled his gaze at David. "No one knows more than I do about the pain and death these mountains have seen. But I've been here a lot longer than you. And I'm telling you, if you climb up in that pulpit today and preach against the evils of illegal liquor, you won't accomplish what you're hoping for."

"How can you be so sure?" Christy asked. "You've never set foot in that church. You've never heard David preach, either. But I have. And he is a very persuasive speaker."

"I'm no theologian," the doctor said. He pushed his tray aside once again, dropping the napkin over his now cold oatmeal. "But I know that when you accuse people, a wall goes up. The last thing they're interested in then is changing their views. All they do is crouch behind that wall to defend themselves."

"Sometimes that's true," David said, "but just the same, I have to try."

The doctor ran his hand through his messy hair. "There's something you two need to understand. Back in these mountains, there's only one real source of money, and that's the sale of good whiskey to outsiders. These people need food and clothes and medicine. How else are they going to get it?"

"But that's not the only way!" Christy cried in frustration. "They could come to us—to the mission—for help."

The doctor shook his head. "Too proud. That's not the way of these folks. They don't want charity."

Silence fell. Christy looked over at David. He seemed as frustrated by the doctor's words as she was.

"Well, I need to get over to the church. I'll see you there, Christy," David said curtly. "Glad you're doing better, Doctor."

"David?" the doctor said.

"Yes?"

"Be careful what you say. Or you may live to regret it." He paused. "As a friend, I'm warning you."

David's eyes flashed. He opened his mouth to speak, then seemed to think the better of it. He left briskly, slamming the door behind him.

A moment later, there was a knock on the door. Ruby Mae poked her head inside. "Miz Christy?" she asked. "You about ready to head on to church?"

"In a minute, Ruby Mae."

Ruby Mae gave a little wave to the doctor. "How'd you like the oatmeal, Doctor? I helped Miss Ida do it up for you. Put my own special fixin's in."

"It had a . . . unique . . . flavor," said Dr. MacNeill.

Ruby Mae grinned at Christy. "Knew he'd like it," she said.

"Ruby Mae, did you wash up the breakfast dishes, like Miss Ida reminded you to?" Christy asked.

Ruby Mae pursed her lips. "No'm, I can't rightly say that I did. I had to give this nice bran mash I made to Prince, on account of him winning the race and all. By the way, Doctor, your horse is doin' fine, too, though I 'spect he misses you. I gave him a little bran mash too."

Christy sighed. "Those dishes—"

"Won't wash themselves, yes'm, I know. Miss Ida tells me that all the time. I'll do 'em as soon as church is over."

"All right, then. Wait for me in the parlor. I'll be right down."

As the door closed behind Ruby Mae, Christy stared at the doctor's white bandage. It brought back vivid memories of the dark blood, the gaping hole, and the look of pain in the doctor's eyes as she'd removed the bullet. A feeling of anger seared through her. "I don't understand you," she muttered.

"Many women have tried," the doctor joked, but Christy was not amused.

"It's only by the grace of God that you're alive, Neil," Christy said in a hushed voice, barely controlling her anger. "How can you see the enemy and not want to fight back?"

"'The enemy'?"

"Moonshine, of course. Illegal liquor and the drunkenness and the feuding that come with it."

The doctor gave her a weary smile. "I wish it were that simple, Christy. But the enemy is much bigger. It's ignorance. And poverty." He closed his eyes. "And that," he added, "is an enemy you are not going to defeat with one sermon."

The service was well under way, and as far as Ruby Mae was concerned, the fun part—the singing and foot tapping and clapping—was done. Now the preacher was speaking.

Ruby Mae sat in one of the front pews. Miz Ida sat on one side, her hands folded primly in her lap. Miz Christy sat on the other. She had a far-off look in her eyes, as if she were figuring something complicated, like one of those math problems Rob Allen liked to work on so much.

Of course, Miz Christy was big on thinking. Ruby Mae knew, because she'd taken a peek at Miz Christy's diary a while back. It was full of big thoughts, deep as the well in the mission yard. Miz Christy had been mad as a plucked hen when she'd caught Ruby Mae reading it, but she'd forgiven her eventually.

She'd even given Ruby Mae a diary of her own to write in. What she wrote, though, wasn't what you'd call deep. Mostly,

Ruby Mae just wrote about how wonderful Prince was. Once or twice she'd even written about Rob Allen's dimples.

Ruby Mae craned her neck, scanning the rows behind her. The preacher was just getting to speechifying, and she didn't want to be rude. But still, she was curious about whether Rob was here today.

She saw her ma and nodded. Ruby Mae was surprised to see her step-pa there too. He hardly ever came to church. He always said, "I don't take no stock in a brought-on city fellow comin' here, a-telling us how to live." Maybe her ma had dragged him here today to show he was sorry for shooting the doctor and all.

Just then Ruby Mae caught sight of Rob sitting at a desk in the back corner. She gave a little wave, and he waved back.

Miz Ida elbowed her hard in the ribs. "Behave, Ruby Mae," she scolded.

Ruby Mae sighed. Between Miz Alice, Miz Christy, and Miz Ida, you couldn't take a breath without one of them telling you how and when and why.

She focused her gaze on the preacher. His face was red, and his eyes burned. He pounded his fist on the pulpit.

Maybe she was missing something. He always talked mighty pretty, about God and love and such things, but she wasn't much on listening to preaching.

Still, there was a strange kind of silence in the church today. The usual coughing and shifting and baby crying had stopped. The only sound was the shuffling of the pigs who often slept under the floorboards in the crawl space. The room was as still and waiting as the moment before a storm comes.

"Some of you," the preacher was saying, "feel that after a

minister has finished his Sunday service, he should shut his eyes to everything going on outside the church. 'Mind your own business,' I have been told."

The preacher paused, gazing out at the crowded room. "Now, in the last twenty-four hours, I've done a lot of thinking about what Jesus's attitude would be toward us here in Cutter Gap, right now in 1912. You'll recall that Jesus said, 'Everyone that doeth evil hateth the light lest his deeds should be reproved. But he that doeth truth cometh to the light.'" The preacher took a deep breath. "He also said, 'No man can serve two masters.' In other words, you can't serve Christ on Sunday and then serve evil on Monday. That is just not possible."

A long silence followed. Suddenly, the preacher pounded the pulpit with his fist again, and Ruby Mae jumped.

"Men and women," he cried, "in this Cove there are those who are working at night—in the darkness—and they are serving evil!"

His voice rang out, climbing into the high rafters. People shifted and murmured. What did he mean, Ruby Mae wondered. What evil? She looked over at Miz Christy for an answer, but her teacher's eyes were glued on the preacher.

"Yesterday, we saw the truth of what I'm saying," the preacher continued, his voice lowered to a near whisper. "We had a celebration—a celebration for a woman, Miss Alice Henderson, who has devoted her life to doing God's work. There was a race, you may recall."

The preacher fixed his gaze on Ruby Mae, and she felt prickles travel the length of her spine. Was he mad at her? Was she somehow doing evil? Sure, she'd been shirking her chores, but was that enough of a sin to get the preacher so all-fired angry?

"Ruby Mae Morrison surprised us all by winning," the preacher continued. He smiled right at her, and she relaxed a little.

"And then," his voice boomed, "a shot rang out, and a man—an innocent man—nearly lost his life."

The preacher moved away from the pulpit. He walked down the aisle separating the two halves of the room. Ruby Mae had never seen him so angry. It scared her. Judging from the looks of others in the room, it scared them too. Some people even looked a little angry.

"The liquor being brewed hereabouts is the devil's own brew," the preacher said. "You know and I know that it leads to fights and killings. Christ meant for our actions on Sunday and every other day to be alike. Don't make the mistake, men and women, of underestimating Him. Our God cannot lose. He will not lose the fight against evil in this Cove, or anywhere in our world!"

Suddenly there was a scraping sound, as a pew was pushed back across the wooden floor. Ruby Mae turned to see Jubal McSween jump to his feet. Jubal, she knew, was one of the Cove men who made moonshine. His face twitched angrily. He looked as if he might say something, but instead he just slammed his hat down on his head and stormed out through the door.

The preacher's face was flushed, his eyes glowing, as he watched Jubal depart. "How many of you want to be on the Lord's side?" he demanded. "Do you?" He pointed his finger out into the crowd. "And you? How about you?"

No one moved. His voice echoed in the silent room. A baby sobbed softly. Ruby Mae felt someone move beside her. She looked up to see Miz Christy, standing proud and tall.

"I do," she said.

On the other side of her, Ruby Mae felt Miz Ida stand. "And so do I," she called out.

Ruby Mae hesitated. No one else was standing. The whole room seemed to be holding its breath.

Her knees trembling, Ruby Mae slowly stood. Miz Christy smiled down at her. "I do," Ruby Mae called out in a voice that seemed thin and puny in the huge room.

She glanced back. Her ma was staring at her with a face that showed no emotion.

Just then, her step-pa climbed to his feet. He sent a cold look toward the preacher. Ruby Mae knew that angry stare far too well.

"Best stay out of other folks' affairs, Preacher," Mr. Morrison warned. "Next time I fire off my rifle, it may not be no accident."

One by one, several other men stood and followed Ruby Mae's stepfather out the door.

## Five

THAT EVENING, CHRISTY RETRIEVED HER DIARY BEFORE crawling into bed. It was late and she was tired, but she wanted to sort out her complicated feelings about the past day.

And it had been a very long day. The doctor, feverish and grumpy, was proving to be a difficult patient. Nothing was ever right. His sheets were tangled. His tea was cold. His dinner was bland. He was bored. He wanted to go home to his own cabin. He had work to do.

But that was just a minor concern. Ida and Miss Alice could handle Dr. MacNeill.

It was David's sermon that had Christy so worried. She was afraid that his stern words had just served to drive away the people he'd hoped to win over. After the service, she'd sensed them staying far away, just as the doctor had warned. Even among those who had stayed through the service, the usual happy chatter had been replaced with terse goodbyes and sullen stares. Obviously, feelings ran very deep on the subject of illegal liquor.

Christy uncapped her pen and began to write:

*April 7, 1912*

*I'm so worried. Miss Alice and David have often warned me that these beautiful mountains are full of danger, and that these wonderful people are capable of dark and dangerous acts. But these past couple of days, I've begun to see it for myself.*

*During David's sermon today about the evils of moonshine, several men stormed out. And afterward there was a tension in the air I've never felt before.*

*The doctor says David and I are too new to Cutter Gap to understand these people. He says we shouldn't interfere. But yesterday I was the one who had to remove a bullet from that man's shoulder—a bullet that wouldn't have been there without the help of liquor. Doesn't that give me a right to an opinion? How can it be wrong to try to change a hurtful thing?*

*And the illegal liquor that is everywhere here is a hurtful thing. I have only to remember the sound of that gunfire, or the sight of Dr. MacNeill's blood-stained shirt, to know that much.*

*Still, I feel uneasy. I can't say why, exactly. But something about the look in the faces of those mountain people, even more than Duggin Morrison's outright threat, makes me feel like we haven't seen the last of the trouble over moonshine.*

Christy set her pen down on the bedside stand. The light from her kerosene lamp flickered. Writing down her thoughts wasn't making her feel any better.

Maybe she should take a walk. Besides, it wouldn't hurt to check on the doctor. His fever had been higher tonight. That wasn't unusual, Miss Alice had said. But she wanted to keep a close eye on him. She'd refused his many demands to let him go back to his own cabin.

Christy put on her robe and slippers and stepped into the hallway, carrying her lamp. She walked down to the doctor's room. The door was ajar. She peered in. His eyes were closed. Asleep, he almost looked sweet and boyish—nothing like the stubborn, annoying man he could be when wide awake.

She tiptoed inside and set the lamp on the dresser. The doctor's forehead was bathed in sweat. She wondered if his fever had gone up. Quietly, she soaked a cloth in the basin of water near his bed.

As she reached over to place the cloth on his forehead, he opened his eyes. "I was having this wonderful dream," he murmured. "This beautiful angel tiptoed into my room to take care of me. Now I see it wasn't a dream."

Christy smiled. "You're still running a fever. Perhaps you're delirious. Is there anything I can get you?"

"My own bed to sleep in."

"Sorry. Miss Alice says you're stuck here for a while longer." Christy retrieved the lamp, then hesitated near the door. "Neil?" she asked softly. "Do you really think David made a mistake, giving that sermon today?"

"From the way you described it to me, yes, I do," the doctor answered gravely.

"Well, I think you're wrong."

"Why did you ask me, then?"

Christy sighed. There was no point in having this conversation. "Goodnight, Doctor."

"Christy?"

"Yes?"

"Don't let Ruby Mae help with breakfast tomorrow, promise?"

Back in the hallway, Christy noticed that Ruby Mae's door was open. She peeked inside. The bed was empty.

Where could that girl be in the middle of the night? Grabbing a midnight snack, perhaps? There were still a few pieces of Miss Alice's birthday cake left. No doubt Ruby Mae had taken it upon herself to finish them off.

Christy headed downstairs. The kitchen was empty. So was the parlor. Strange. Where on earth could Ruby Mae have gone, unless . . . Christy smiled. Of course.

She put the lamp aside and stepped outside. It was still very cold at night. The mountains took their sweet time warming up to spring, Fairlight Spencer liked to say.

Christy walked quickly across the wet lawn, shivering in her thin robe. Miss Alice's cabin was dark. David's bunkhouse wasn't visible from here. Christy wondered if he were having trouble sleeping too. He'd seemed as surprised as she'd been by the hot rage and the icy silence that had greeted his sermon.

The little shed that housed Prince, Miss Alice's horse, Goldie, and the mission's crippled mule, Old Theo, was just past the schoolhouse. Christy was almost there when she heard an odd shuffling noise. It seemed to be coming from the crawl space under the schoolhouse.

She paused, listening. Nothing. Probably just the hogs who lived under there. It had taken her a while to get used to the notion of teaching in a one-room schoolhouse with hogs as downstairs neighbors. Once they had even gotten loose in her classroom, causing quite a commotion.

When she reached the shed, Christy swung open the wooden door. It let out a tired creak.

"Who's there?" came a frightened voice.

"Don't worry, Ruby Mae, it's just me, Miss Christy."

Ruby was sitting in Prince's stall. He was lying down in the sweet-smelling hay. A patch of moonlight, coming from the only window, streaked his velvet side. Ruby Mae sat next to him, a horse blanket over her legs. Her diary was nearby.

"Miz Christy!" she exclaimed. "You nearly scared me to death!"

"I'm sorry." Christy joined her in the stall. The hay was prickly and warm. Prince gazed at her sleepily, clearly wondering why he was getting so many late-night visitors. "I couldn't sleep, and then I saw you were gone and got worried."

"Well, I'm glad it's just you. I thought I was hearin' noises before," Ruby Mae said.

"Probably just the hogs. Or the wind," Christy said. She stroked Prince's soft muzzle. "Do you sneak out here often?"

"Some," Ruby Mae said guardedly.

"You love Prince a lot, don't you?"

"More'n anything in the whole wide world, I reckon." Ruby Mae pulled a piece of straw out of her curly hair. "More'n my ma and step-pa, even, I sometimes think. Is that wrong, Miz Christy, to feel like that?"

"You're just going through a rough time with your parents right now, Ruby Mae. It'll pass."

Ruby Mae sighed. "I hope you're right. But my step-pa looked right mad at me today, after that sermon by the preacher. After church he told me I was getting carried away, living here at the mission. Said he might even make me come back home to live." She sighed. "My step-pa thinks people like you and the preacher are pokin' in where you don't belong. He said there'd be trouble if'n you didn't tend to your own business."

"Do you think a lot of people feel that way?" Christy asked.

"Reckon so. It's just the way folks is, Miz Christy. They get set in their ways, and they don't like gettin' un-set, if you follow my meanin'. Preacher, he's maybe goin' too fast . . . not that I got any right to say."

Christy leaned back against the rough, cool wood of the wall. She pointed to Ruby Mae's diary and smiled. "I was writing in my diary too."

"What did you say?" Ruby Mae asked. Her hand flew to her mouth. "Oops. I forgot how they're private-like. You don't have to tell me. But I'll tell you mine. I was writin' how when I'm here with Prince, it seems like the whole rest of the world can just float away for all I care. I was writin' about this place we go to, over past Blackberry Creek. There's a spot—a cave, like—where we just sit and watch the world a-spinnin', and I think actual thoughts sometimes."

Christy smiled. "Actual thoughts? I'm very impressed."

"I mean, I know I ain't no John Spencer or Rob Allen or nothin'." She laughed. "My step-pa says I have chicken feathers for brains. But still, I think sometimes." She hesitated. "You think someone as all-fired smart as Rob could ever hanker after someone with feathers for brains?"

"Of course he could. But don't you ever say that about yourself, Ruby Mae. I've probably learned as much about the Cove from you as I have from Miss Alice."

"Truly?"

"Truly. Of course, I wouldn't mind if you paid a little more attention to your studies and chores and a little less attention to Prince."

"But can't you see why?" Ruby Mae asked. She hugged Prince's neck. "Isn't bein' here just the plumb best place in the whole world?

Christy nodded. "You're right. It just may be."

Using Prince's broad back for a pillow, Ruby Mae stretched out in the hay. Christy joined her, and together they covered themselves with the scratchy, horse-smelling blanket. The little window on the far wall gave them a tiny square of sky to look at.

"Peaceful-like, ain't it?" Ruby Mae whispered.

Staring up at the little patch of star-studded sky, it did seem peaceful. Guns and moonshine and anger seemed very, very far away indeed. Christy rested her cheek on Prince's warm, soft back, and let herself drift into a restless sleep.

⌒#⌒

"Ruby Mae, could you come over here, please?" Christy called the next afternoon. Recess was over, and the children were reluctantly heading back into the classroom.

They all had a bad case of spring fever, Christy had decided. She'd had a hard time getting anyone to pay attention to her lesson on the American Revolution that morning. There had been a lot of daydreaming going on. Still, no one seemed to be shirking schoolwork more than Ruby Mae. And Christy had a feeling it wasn't the fine early spring weather that was the culprit. It was a certain black stallion by the name of Prince.

"Yes, Miz Christy?" Ruby Mae called. She and Rob Allen

were sauntering toward the school. Ruby Mae's cheeks were flushed, and she was grinning from ear to ear.

*Well*, Christy thought, *maybe Prince isn't the only distraction in Ruby Mae's life.*

"I need to talk to you for a minute, Ruby Mae," Christy said. "Privately."

Rob cleared his throat. "I'll head on inside," he said quickly, giving Ruby Mae a shy smile.

Christy led Ruby Mae away from the school into the cool shade of a large oak.

"Don't he just have the cutest little dimples you ever did see?" Ruby Mae asked.

"Ruby Mae," Christy said, "we need to talk. I graded your history test during recess. And it was not a pretty sight. Did you even read the assignment I gave the class?"

Ruby Mae gulped. "I sort of . . . shinnied over it, quick-like. Truth to tell, it was dull as dishwater."

Christy leaned against the oak, her arms crossed over her chest. "Speaking of dishwater, Miss Ida told me you shinnied over the breakfast dishes this morning too."

"I was groomin' Prince. He ain't had a proper hoof pickin' in days. Stones get caught in there, and it hurts somethin' fierce if'n—"

"Ruby Mae, I'm afraid I'm going to have to take away your riding privileges for a while. For the next few weeks, David will take care of Prince, until your grades improve and you start paying attention to your chores."

"But—but you just can't take away Prince, Miz Christy!" Ruby Mae cried, so loudly that some of the students peered out the windows to see what all the commotion was about. "He's the most important thing in the world to me! I promise

I'll work on my grades and read my history, even if it is borin'. And I'll do my chores proper-like. Only you just can't take Prince away from me! I'll like to die if'n you do."

Christy touched Ruby Mae's shoulder, but the girl yanked away angrily. "It's not forever, Ruby Mae. Just for a little while. It's for your own good. Miss Alice and David and I discussed it this morning."

"What do you all know about my own good?" Ruby Mae screamed. Tears streamed down her freckled cheeks. "Prince needs me. And I need him! You . . . you saw how it was, last night. I thought you understood."

"I do understand," Christy said gently. "It isn't like he's going away, Ruby Mae. He'll be right here at the mission, if you want to say hello." She sighed. "I'm sorry to have to do this, Ruby Mae, but the sooner you get back on track, the sooner you can spend time with Prince again."

Ruby Mae stared at her in disbelief, her eyes glistening with tears. She opened her mouth, as if to argue, then gave up, spun on her heel and dashed into the school.

"What's with Ruby Mae?"

Christy turned to see David crossing the lawn with his usual long, determined stride. He was carrying the textbook he used for the math class he taught in the afternoon.

"She's furious about our decision. Poor thing. I feel so bad for her. But she's got to keep up with her schoolwork." Christy shook her head. "It's hard being the disciplinarian. Just a few months ago, my parents were telling me what to do—trying, anyway. I'm not used to being the bad guy."

"Then you can imagine how I felt yesterday telling my whole congregation to stop doing something that they insist is their God-given right." David gazed back at the mission house. "The doctor and I had another argument this morning. He insisted I shouldn't have given that sermon. And that the reception it got shouldn't have surprised me."

"And what did you say?" Christy asked.

"I told him to mind his own business—"

"To which he said you should be minding yours," Christy finished his explanation.

David gave a grim smile. "You do know how the doctor's mind works, don't you?"

"Yes." Christy laughed.

Just then she heard a low grunt coming from the rear of the school. One of the hogs who resided under the building sauntered out into the sunshine, making its way along the side of the school.

"Looks like Mabel's up from her nap," Christy said, pointing to the big hog.

"Mabel?"

"Creed Allen named her. Says she looks like his great-aunt Mabel over in Big Gap—except for the tail, of course."

"I'll wager that Mabel's the only one who heard my sermon yesterday and didn't mind it."

"I thought it was a very fine sermon," Christy said.

"Thanks—" David began, then paused. "Am I crazy, or is that hog walking a bit oddly?"

They watched as Mabel took a few faltering steps. She walked on a slant, as if she were fighting a stiff wind.

"Very strange," Christy murmured. "Maybe she's sick. Let's go check it out."

As they approached the side of the school, Christy noticed an intense, almost sickeningly sweet, medicine-like odor. Toward the back of the building, she stumbled over a broken jug. Nearby were several hogs, stretched out asleep—very asleep. As Christy and David approached, they did not stir. They were breathing heavily.

David stared at the pigs. He gently poked first one and then another with his foot, but they just kept snoring.

"This is very odd," Christy said. The hogs never slept this soundly. Usually, she could hear them snuffling and rooting around under the building while she taught.

"I don't get it." David stooped to look under the floor. "It's almost too dark to see anything. I'll have to go in under there."

He crouched over, slowly making his way under the building. Christy could hear his fingers groping, then some boards being moved.

Suddenly he gave a loud whistle. "Christy, you should see this!" he cried, his voice filled with amazement and anger.

# Six

Christy knelt down. "What is it, David?"

"Jugs, lots of them! Moonshine whiskey! I should have recognized the smell."

"But . . . right here, underneath the school?" Christy cried in disbelief.

She heard voices and turned to see several of her students. Ruby Mae hung back from the group. Her face was red and blotchy from crying.

"Miz Christy," asked Creed Allen. "What in tarnation is wrong with all these hogs? Mabel's walkin' like she's got her legs screwed on backwards. And the rest of 'em—well, I ain't never heard this much hog-snorin' in all my days!"

"Christy," David called from under the school, "can you take these jugs from me? I'll hand them to you, one at a time."

"Just a minute, David. Some of the children are here—"

"Let them see!" David called angrily. "Let them see the evil hidden under their own schoolhouse."

"What's hidden?" asked Little Burl Allen, Creed's sweet

six-year-old brother. "Is the preacher a-playin' hide-and-seek, Teacher?"

"Not exactly, Little Burl," Christy said just as David passed her a thick brown jug. She set it on the ground. The children stared at it curiously.

"Moonshine?" whispered John Spencer, one of the older students.

"There's moonshine under the school?" Creed cried. "No wonder them hogs is snorin' so loud! They's drunk on home-made whiskey!"

Most of the children began to laugh, although a few of the older boys, like Lundy Taylor, kept watching Christy guardedly.

"I know it seems funny," Christy said as she accepted more jugs from David. "But this is no laughing matter, children."

"I'll say it ain't," Lundy muttered darkly. "My pa says you-all are messin' where you don't belong. This ain't the business of a teacher or a preacher person."

David crawled out from under the floor space, his face smudged with dirt. His eyes were hot with anger.

"I heard that, Lundy," he said as he stood. "And let me tell you something you can pass on to your pa. When I find illegal liquor on mission property, it becomes my business, whether your pa and his friends like it or not."

David stooped down and grabbed one of the jugs. He uncorked it and sniffed the contents with a look of disgust. Then he turned the jug upside down. The amber liquid gurgled and spattered as it poured onto the ground. The air filled with a sharp, sweet smell.

"You ain't got no right to throw away good moonshine like that!" Lundy cried.

"There's nothing good about moonshine, Lundy Taylor," Christy said with feeling. "Didn't you see what happened to Dr. MacNeill?"

"But ain't that worth a lot of money, Teacher?" Creed asked innocently. "Pa says moonshine fetches a big price, 'specially over the state lines where it's hard to get."

"It's also worth a lot of pain, Creed," Christy said.

David uncorked another bottle. His hands trembled. Christy had never seen him so furious.

"Children, I want you all to go back inside now," she instructed.

"But what about them hogs?" Little Burl asked, worried.

"They'll sleep it off, Little Burl," Christy assured him, patting his tangled hair. "Don't you worry."

"When my grandpa gets to drinkin', he'll sleep for two days straight," said Bessie Coburn.

"Yes, well, we can talk about that more inside," Christy said, shooing the children away. Slowly they returned to class, until only Lundy was left. He was a big boy, almost as tall as David. And with the threatening look in his eyes right now, he seemed even bigger.

"Do you know anything about who put these jugs here, Lundy?" Christy asked, her voice quivering.

Lundy glared at her. "I ain't a-tellin' you nothin' except this: you mission folks is makin' a big mistake."

"Don't you go threatening us, Lundy Taylor," David warned.

"We have to get rid of the moonshine, Lundy," Christy said gently yet firmly. "Can't you see that?"

Lundy backed away slowly. "All I see is a heap more trouble than the sorry likes of you can handle."

Without another word, he raced off into the thick woods.

"I still don't understand why they put the moonshine there," Christy said at dinner that night. "Right under the church! It's such a crazy place to store illegal liquor."

Silence fell over the table. It had been a tense meal. David was still fuming about the moonshine. Ruby Mae was still pouting about Prince. Dr. MacNeill, who'd insisted on coming downstairs to join them for dinner, was still running a fever. Miss Alice was gathering up supplies. She was on her way to help a woman in Big Gap deliver a baby. And Miss Ida was annoyed that no one was eating the meal she'd prepared.

"I wonder how long those jugs have been down there," Christy continued.

"They may have put them there long ago," David suggested, "thinking it would be the last place anyone would look. Or it could have been a defiant gesture—an answer, if you can call it that, to my sermon last Sunday."

"Come to think of it, I did hear noises out by the school late last night," Christy said.

"You were outside last night?" David asked in surprise.

Christy glanced over at Ruby Mae. "Oh, just for a few minutes. A little walk to clear my head."

David looked over at the doctor. "I suppose, with this latest development, you're dying to say I told you so?"

Dr. MacNeill shifted positions in his chair. He'd barely touched his food. "No, David," he said after a moment of reflection. "I'm not about to gloat. What would be the point?"

"Since when do you keep your opinions to yourself?" David demanded.

The doctor sighed heavily. "I will tell you this: I am

worried about this situation. It was one thing to preach a sermon about moonshine. It was quite another to dump out jug after jug. That was someone's property, like it or not—"

"Property!" David cried. "That was illegal liquor, on my property!" He paused. "On our property, I should say."

"That's not the point," the doctor said. "The point is that you've just added fuel to a very dangerous fire. I'm worried that whoever put that moonshine there will try to retaliate now."

"Retaliate?" Miss Ida echoed. "Against whom?"

"Against the mission. Against David, or maybe Christy. After all, the children witnessed them dumping the moonshine together."

David looked at Christy and frowned. "I'm the one who did the dumping and gave the sermon. Why would they act against Christy?"

"Because she represents the mission too," the doctor answered. "In a way, she has more contact with these people than you do. You see them every Sunday for an hour, if you're lucky. She's the one teaching the children of these moonshiners every single day."

The doctor winced as he tried to reach for a glass of water. Ruby Mae moved it closer for him. "Thanks, Ruby Mae. Say, you've been awfully quiet this evening."

Ruby Mae stared at her plate, her lower lip jutting.

"She's pouting," Christy explained.

"And why is that?" asked Dr. MacNeill.

"They won't let me take care of Prince anymore and he's just gonna plain starve out there without me!" Ruby Mae cried.

"Ruby Mae," David said gently, "I fed Prince an hour ago.

He ate like . . . well, like a horse. Trust me. He is not going to starve."

"Without me, he's a-goin' to starve for love!" Ruby Mae cried.

Christy smiled at the doctor. "Tell us, Doctor. Have you ever come across such a medical condition?"

"Starving for love. Hmmm." The doctor tapped his finger on his chin. "There have been documented cases, although they usually appear in the human male." He grinned at Christy. "Now, in a mammal the size of a horse, I would think it would take, oh, a good two months or so for any symptoms to develop."

"Two months," Christy repeated, winking at the doctor. "That's plenty of time for you to get your schoolwork and chores back on track, Ruby Mae."

"What does he know?" Ruby Mae said. "He ain't no horse doctor."

"By the way, have you started on that English homework I assigned?" Christy asked.

"Not yet," Ruby Mae said sullenly.

Miss Alice came bustling into the room from the kitchen, where she had packed some food to take with her. She carried a paper sack and her medical bag in her left hand. Her sprained wrist was much better, but she still had her right arm in a sling most of the time.

She pursed her lips. "I do hate to go, what with Neil still running a fever and this trouble with the moonshine. But Janey Cook's had a couple of hard deliveries, and I'd like to be there. I won't be as much use as I'd like, with this arm of mine, but her grandmother will be there too. Together we should manage."

"Be careful, Miss Alice," the doctor warned. "I'm concerned about retaliation over that moonshine David threw out."

"I can take care of myself," Miss Alice said. She shook a warning finger at the group. "But I want the rest of you to keep an eye out. And David, this might be a good time to let things simmer down a little. Give folks a chance to think."

"Who is it you think is going to be retaliating, anyway?" David asked, sounding defensive.

"Bird's-Eye Taylor is one of the biggest moonshiners in these parts, of course," Miss Alice said. "And I suspect he uses Lundy to help him. But there are others."

"Tom McHone, for one," the doctor added. "And Jubal McSween and Dug—" He stopped in midsentence.

"Go ahead and say it, Doc," said Ruby Mae, her eyes flashing. "Sure, my step-pa's made moonshine and sold it some. Everybody does it around these parts. I ain't defendin' him or nothin'. But there ain't no way else to make a proper living here." She tossed her napkin onto the table. "Not like that'll stop you all from tellin' the rest of the world how to live their lives and what they can do and can't do and if'n they can be with the one thing that means more to them than the whole rest of the wide world." She pushed back her chair. "Can I be excused?" she demanded. "I got dishes to do, and homework."

"Yes, Ruby Mae," Christy said. "You may be excused."

She watched as Ruby Mae dashed from the room. "I hope she doesn't stay mad forever," she said sadly.

"That's one thing people in these mountains do very, very well," said the doctor with a weary smile. "Stay mad. And get even."

Ruby Mae stared down at the tear-stained diary page. The ink was blurry. The letters melted one into another, but she could still make out her words:

> I can't stand it no more. It just ain't fare. Prins needs me as much as I need him. Well, mebbe not as much, but almost. Itz only bin a few ours and my hart is braking. How kin I go for weeks without seein him, or mebbe even longer?

She wiped her eyes and sniffled. It was very late. The others had gone to sleep hours ago.

With a sigh, she went to the window and opened it wide. The chill air sent a shiver through her. Out there, past Miss Alice's vegetable garden, past the lattice-covered well, past the school, was the little shed where Prince waited for her.

Did he miss her as much as she missed him? Creed Allen said animals could feel even more than people could, and she liked to think he was right. (Although Creed also swore that his raccoon, Scalawag, could read his mind, and she had serious doubts about that. After all, Creed was known for the whoppers he liked to tell.)

A sound—a strange, rhythmic thud—met her ears. It seemed to be coming from far away, but there was an urgency to it.

Ruby Mae listened, straining to make out the source of the sound. It was coming from the direction of the schoolhouse. Could it be someone had returned to put more moonshine under the school? She hoped not, especially since it wouldn't surprise her to learn her step-pa was involved. Truth was she didn't rightly see what business it was of the preacher and Miz Christy if her step-pa wanted to make moonshine. But she sure didn't want them getting riled up all over again.

Suddenly, she heard a wild, desperate whinny, like nothing she'd ever heard before.

Prince! It had to be him.

The sound came again, a horrible cry carried on the wind. He sounded terribly afraid. Whatever was happening to Prince, it was bad, very bad. She had to get to him, and get there fast.

Ruby Mae threw open her bedroom door and flew down the stairs. She ran across the wet lawn in her bare feet. Another terrified whinny filled the air, followed by a series of pounding noises, as if Prince were trying to kick right through the sides of his stall.

She didn't slow down, not for an instant, not even when she realized that there might be someone lurking behind the dark trees, lying in wait.

Breathless and shivering, she finally made it to the shed. The door was slightly ajar. Either the preacher had forgotten to close the door, or someone else had been here.

*Or someone might even still be here.*

With a deep breath, Ruby Mae flung open the door. "Who's there?" she cried, trying her best to sound like someone big and scary and well armed.

She took a step inside. The familiar smells of hay and leather and manure greeted her. In the dim moonlight she could make out something lying on the floor.

It was the preacher's saddle, the one Prince wore. Ruby Mae knelt down, tracing her fingers over the dark leather. Someone had slashed the beautiful saddle with a knife. Long gashes covered the seat. The girth had been ripped out and tossed aside.

A low, sweet whinny of greeting made Ruby Mae look up. "Prince?" she whispered. "Are you all right, boy?"

Trembling, she stepped closer. And then she saw the answer to her question. The beautiful black stallion was not all right. Not at all.

# Seven

"LORDAMERCY!" RUBY MAE CRIED IN HORROR. "PRINCE, what have they done to you?"

Prince's beautiful flowing tail, mane, and forelock had been sheared off. They lay clumped in the hay by his feet. He looked pathetic, and he knew it. He pawed at the floor, throwing his head up and down in angry protest.

Ruby Mae draped her arms around the horse's broad neck. "Oh, Prince," she moaned, "I could just bust out cryin'. You ain't hurt, is you?"

Carefully she ran her hands over his shoulders and flanks and legs, searching for any cuts or wounds. As far as she could tell, there were none. But the loss of his gorgeous mane and tail was insult enough.

"Ruby Mae?" a voice called frantically.

Miz Christy ran into the shed. She carried a lantern. Seconds later, Dr. MacNeill and the preacher appeared behind her.

"We heard your scream—" Miz Christy began. Her eyes fell on the saddle. "What happened?"

"Prince!" David cried, rushing over to the agitated stallion. "What's happened here, Ruby Mae?"

Ruby Mae knelt down and picked up a handful of Prince's silky tail. "I'll tell you what happened," she cried. "Someone hurt Prince to get back at you. If you'da just kept quiet about the moonshine, this would never have happened! It's your fault, Preacher." She turned to Miz Christy. "And your fault too. Why couldn't you all have left well enough alone?"

She was crying, but she couldn't stop herself. Hot tears spilled down her cheeks. She buried her face in Prince's neck, and he seemed to calm down, as if he understood that she needed him.

"Are the others all right?" the preacher asked. "Old Theo and Bill?"

Dr. MacNeill looked over the old mule and his own horse. "They're fine," he said, "just a little nervous, what with all the commotion." He stroked Prince's muzzle. "Looks like they didn't waste any time getting even," he said grimly. "It's like I said, David. Revenge is the way of the mountains."

"So this is my fault?" the preacher cried. "I'm responsible for this horrible act?"

"I'm not saying that," said the doctor. "I'm just saying it's time to back off. Call a truce. Let the highlanders have their moonshine, and you get back to the business of being a preacher."

"This is part of the business of being a preacher." The preacher sighed. "Look, Doctor, I understand your point of view. Really, I do. But you must understand that it's not my job to just tell people what they want to hear. Sometimes it's my job to tell people exactly what they don't want to hear. No matter the cost."

Ruby Mae watched as the preacher tenderly stroked Prince's withers. She could see the pain in the man's dark eyes. Could it be he was as upset as she was?

"You didn't see anyone, did you, Ruby Mae?" he asked softly.

"No, sir."

"You'd tell me if you had, wouldn't you? Even if it was someone you knew?"

"I didn't see my step-pa, if that's what you're gettin' at." Ruby Mae fought back a sob. "I didn't see anyone." She scratched Prince's right ear. He gave a soft nicker, then lay his head on her shoulder.

"He was so purty, with that long mane of his a-sweepin' back in the wind," Ruby Mae said. "And now he looks plumb unnatural, like a mule—no offense to you, Old Theo. He won't even have nothin' to flick off the flies with." A wave of anger washed over her. "I wish I could knock the livin' daylights out of them that done this. Even if it were my own step-pa."

"I can't believe anyone could be this cruel," Miz Christy said in a sad, faraway voice. She was crying, too, Ruby Mae suddenly realized.

"It could have been worse," said the doctor. "They might have injured him, even killed him." The doctor leaned against the wall. He looked weak and pale. "Getting even is considered a virtue around here. The mark of a strong character. Truth is you were lucky this time. They let you off easy."

"Easy?" Miz Christy cried.

"You're sitting on a powder keg, Christy," the doctor said. "It only takes one match to set it off. David came close to it with his sermon."

"No doubt you're right about that, Doctor," the preacher

said, his voice growing angry again. "There is a powder keg here. But you can't simply wish evil away. You have to stand up and oppose it. You know as well as I do that this illegal liquor is behind at least half the terrible things that happen in these mountains. And I don't see you offering any solutions."

"I don't have any easy solutions to offer," the doctor said, rubbing his shoulder gingerly. "I just know that the Cove people don't see anything criminal about making a little homemade brew. After all, it's know-how that's been passed down through their families for generations. To them, it's not a moral issue. Especially when they can't find any other way to make a living here in these mountains."

"But it is a moral issue, Doctor," said Miz Christy. "You're an educated man. You can see it. Moonshining has horrible results—feuds and terror and even death. How can you ignore all that? How can you ignore that painful wound in your own shoulder?"

"I'm not ignoring any of it," the doctor said. His voice was suddenly full of rage. "I've been taking care of these people a whole lot longer than you and David. The two of you come along and decide you're going to tell people how to live their lives. What gives you that right?"

Silence fell. Ruby Mae gulped. She had never heard this kind of grown-up argufying. Sure, her ma and step-pa fought all the time. But those fights were just made of loud words flying around the cabin. This fight was about loud words and big ideas. Ruby Mae wasn't sure she understood everything, but one thing was clear: the doctor and Miz Christy and the preacher were nowhere close to agreeing about moonshine.

"I might as well ask you the same thing, Doctor," the preacher said in a low whisper of a voice. "What gives you the right to condone evil? Are you doing these people a favor by defending their addiction to moonshine? The Bible says we must love the sinner, even though we hate the sin. And by hating the sin, and resisting the sin, perhaps we can help to free the sinner. That's why I preached against moonshine. Not because I don't care about these people, but because I do."

"Well, I'm just one man, doing what little I can to help," the doctor said. "You can't change the world overnight. Unfortunately, you and Christy haven't figured that out yet. I have."

"How can you be so arrogant?" Miz Christy demanded.

Ruby Mae gasped. She wasn't positive what arrogant meant, but she was pretty sure it wasn't the nicest thing in the world you could be.

The doctor started toward the door, then paused. "Funny. I was going to ask you two the same thing." The shed door closed behind him.

"He's awful riled, ain't he?" Ruby Mae whispered.

"We all are," Miz Christy said with a sigh. "Well, there's nothing more we can do here tonight. Come on, Ruby Mae. We'll check on Prince in the morning. He just needs some rest now."

"No!" Ruby Mae cried. "I'm not leavin' him alone."

"You can't stay," the preacher said gently. "It isn't safe out here. I'll keep an ear open for anything unusual. Prince will be fine. I promise."

"Lot of good that'll do me," Ruby Mae said bitterly. "You're the reason we're in this fix." She turned to Miz Christy. She was Ruby Mae's only hope. "Please, Miz Christy. Let me stay here. You know I'll be all right." Tears spilled down Ruby Mae's cheeks. "If'n I'd been here before, Miz Christy, maybe I could have saved Prince."

But Miz Christy just shook her head. "If you'd have been here before, you might have been hurt yourself, Ruby Mae. I'm sorry, but David's right. You head on upstairs. We'll check on Prince in the morning."

"But—"

"No, Ruby Mae. You need your sleep for school tomorrow. And Prince needs to rest up too."

There was no point in fighting them. She was outnumbered. Ruby Mae kissed Prince gently on the muzzle. "You'll be back to your old self in no time, boy," she whispered. "Don't you worry."

Ruby Mae ran back to her room, crying all the way. She was still crying when she finally drifted off to sleep.

⌐#⌐

When Christy got home from school the next afternoon, she found an envelope with her name on it sitting on the dining room table. "What's this?" she called to Miss Ida.

Miss Ida came in from the kitchen, wiping flour-covered hands on her crisp apron. "A note from the doctor."

"A note? But why would he write me a note? Isn't he upstairs?"

Miss Ida shook her head. "He left for home about an hour ago. I tried to stop him. Told him he looked like death warmed over and that you and Miss Alice would be furious. Besides, it appears there's a big storm coming on. But you know the doctor. Stubbornest man that ever laid foot on God's green earth."

"He left?" Christy dropped into a chair, rubbing her eyes. "This is awful. It's all because of the terrible fight we had last night after we found Prince. I wondered why the doctor didn't come down to breakfast this morning. David and I should have tried to resolve things with him."

"You know the doctor was hankering to get back to his own cabin, anyway," Miss Ida said. "He asked me today how I could believe in a merciful God when He allows Ruby Mae to keep making oatmeal."

The front door opened and David rushed inside. He was wearing his work clothes. His shoes were covered with hay and mud. "Anyone seen the doctor?" he asked breathlessly. "I was just putting Prince out in the pasture, and I noticed the doctor's horse is gone!"

Christy held up the envelope. "Dr. MacNeill left about an hour ago."

"Well, that's a relief," David said, sinking into the chair next to Christy.

"David, how can you say that?" Christy demanded.

"I meant it's a relief to know he took his horse," David said. "I was afraid it might have been stolen. You know—the moonshiners up to their tricks again. Although"—he winked at Miss Ida—"I have to admit I won't exactly miss the man."

"The doctor is still sick," Christy insisted. "He should never have left here, especially after our argument last night."

"It's not as if we could have resolved things, Christy," David said. "There are some things people are just never going to agree on."

Christy opened the envelope and read the letter inside:

*My dear Christy:*

*You have been a fine hostess, nurse, and surgeon, but I find I must get back to my patients before you spoil me any further.*

*I trust that David will keep an eye on you, but please be careful in the days ahead. We may argue about many things, David and I, but about you, at least, we seem to be in remarkable agreement.*

*Neil MacNeill*

*P.S. You still owe me a dance.*

Christy set the letter aside. "David, we have to go get him."

"What?" David cried. "Go get the doctor? After what he said to us last night?"

"The point is he's running a high fever."

"He's a doctor," David argued. "He can take better care of himself than we can."

"David. Be reasonable."

He gazed at her pleadingly. "You're not going to budge on this, are you?"

Christy shook her head.

David looked at her intently. "You know, the doctor's cabin is a long ride off. And I can't take Prince. He's way too high strung to be ridden today. I'd never even get a saddle on him."

"Poor thing," Christy said. "I let Ruby Mae and Rob go visit him during the noon recess. Ruby Mae said she'd never seen him so skittish. She's still furious at us, by the way."

"I know. She wouldn't say a word to me during math class this afternoon." David sighed. "The point is I'll have to ride Old Theo. And let's face it, that mule isn't exactly the fastest thing on four legs. Not only that, it looks like it's going to storm."

"Maybe I should go."

"Christy, you know I can't let you do that." David stood

and stretched. "Okay, I'll go get the doctor. Assuming, that is, he'll come back. The man's more ornery than Old Theo."

"Which is why you're the perfect person to retrieve him," Christy said.

David rolled his eyes. "I'll try to make this quick," he said. "With luck, I may even be back before dark. But in the meantime, you and Miss Ida and Ruby Mae stay close to the house, all right?"

"We will," Christy agreed. "But don't you think the danger's past, now that the moonshiners have gotten their revenge?"

"Maybe so, maybe not. On this, at least, I'm inclined to listen to the doctor."

# Eight

Ruby Mae stared at her dinner plate. Usually, she loved Miss Ida's chicken pot pie, but this evening she was in no mood to eat. She was still furious at the preacher and Miz Christy about what had happened to Prince. And since the preacher was out hunting for Dr. MacNeill, that meant the only person Ruby Mae could be mad at for the time being was Miz Christy. They'd barely spoken all through supper, except for the occasional "Pass the muffins" or "May I have the salt?"

Still, Ruby Mae knew that she was only going to get what she wanted if she acted at least a little polite to her teacher. She could be polite on the outside and mad on the inside, she figured.

"Miz Christy," Ruby Mae said, trying on her pretend-sweet voice, "can I go out and check on Prince, seein' as how the preacher's not back yet from fetchin' the doctor? It'll be dark soon, and there's a storm a-brewin'. You know how Prince hates thunder. Gets himself all riled up over it. And I already done finished my math homework before supper."

Miz Christy gave her an I-don't-believe-you look.

"Looky here, I'll prove it to you," Ruby Mae said. She pursed her lips. "Twelve divided by three is five."

"Twelve divided by three is four, Ruby Mae."

"Well, still and all, I was right close."

With a sigh, Miz Christy got up and crossed to the window. The sky was covered with thick, gray clouds. Flashes of far-off lightning lit the horizon, but there was still no sign of rain.

"Actually, it looks like the storm's going to pass us by," Miz Christy said. "It may have stalled to the west, over that next ridge. I wonder if David and the doctor got caught in it. They should be back by now."

"All the more reason I oughta put Prince in the shed for the night, don't you figure?" Ruby Mae pressed. "When the preacher gets back, he'll be mighty tuckered out."

"You've got some dinner dishes to take care of," Miz Christy reminded her.

Ruby Mae felt her heart sink. What good was using her most polite tone of voice, if Miz Christy wasn't even going to have the good sense to notice it?

"I can get to 'em when I get back," Ruby Mae offered.

"All right, then," Christy said. "But make it quick, Ruby Mae. I want you back in twenty minutes, understand? And if you see or hear anything unusual, you hightail it right back here."

"I promise!" Ruby Mae cried with relief as she jumped from her chair. "Twenty minutes and not a lick more."

"Oh, and Ruby Mae? Give these to Prince for me, would you?"

Miz Christy reached into the sugar bowl and passed Ruby Mae a handful of glistening white sugar cubes.

"Christy!" Miz Ida cried. "Do you realize how expensive that sugar is? And you're giving it to a horse?"

"He's not just any horse, Miss Ida," Christy said, smiling at Ruby Mae.

Ruby Mae put the sugar in the pocket of her yellow skirt. "Thanks, Miz Christy," she said gratefully, and for that moment, at least, she wasn't using a pretend voice anymore.

⸻

On her way to the pasture, Ruby Mae tried to figure out what was going on inside her. Her heart felt crowded with way too many feelings, and she didn't like it one bit. She felt the way she did when she tried to do division problems—there was one question, but way too many answers. Maybe her step-pa was right. Maybe she really did have chicken feathers for brains.

She started up the path to the pasture. It led through a thick stand of pines then opened onto the small, cleared area where the mission horses grazed. Way off in the distance, thunder rumbled—a low groan that made it sound like the sky had a bellyache. Miz Christy was probably right. It looked like the storm had moved on. Good thing. Prince hated storms. Always had.

It was hard, staying mad at her teacher. Truth was Ruby Mae liked Miz Christy a whole heap, and the preacher too. They were good people. A little big on dos and don'ts, maybe, but they meant well.

Today during the noon recess, Rob had gone with Ruby Mae to check on Prince. When he saw what had happened to the beautiful stallion, he'd been almost as upset as she'd been. When Ruby Mae had told him how angry she was at the preacher and Miz Christy, Rob had listened very quietly until she'd said her piece. He'd thought for a good, long while before speaking.

"Maybe," he'd said at last, all slow and careful-like, "you're even madder at your own self, Ruby Mae. You wanted to take care of Prince, and you couldn't. Maybe you feel kinda like you let him down."

He was right, of course. That's why Rob was such a smart boy. He could look right at someone and see straight into their heart.

Rob had said something else too. He'd told Ruby Mae she shouldn't let herself feel bad. That Prince was the luckiest horse in the world to have her for a friend.

She wasn't so sure Rob was right about that. But it had made her feel better, just the same.

As Ruby Mae neared the end of the path, she let out a whistle for Prince. It was a little game they had. He would hear her whistle and gallop over to greet her. By the time she emerged from the stand of pines, he'd be waiting by the fence, tossing his head and snorting and carrying on. Of course, she wasn't sure he'd respond to her whistle today. He hadn't been his usual playful self when she'd gone to visit him at recess. He'd seemed jittery, skittish, and afraid of the least little thing.

The path through the pines ended and the pasture came into view. Ruby Mae leapt onto the split-rail fence that the preacher had built to surround the small grassy area.

"Hey, boy—" she began, and then her heart turned cold as stone.

Prince was gone! Even in the twilight gloom, she could tell that he was nowhere in the pasture.

She scrambled over the fence, frantic with fear. "Prince!"

she screamed, running through the grass. "Where are you, boy?"

Then she saw the spot. At the far end of the fence, a top rail had been knocked loose. She knew what had happened. Prince had bolted over the fence. Maybe he'd been scared off by the thunder. Maybe he'd just been so upset over what had happened to him that he'd run away out of pure embarrassment.

Or maybe someone had chased Prince off, or even stolen him.

Ruby Mae checked the sky. It was nearly dark, but she had to find Prince. She figured she was going to be in a world of trouble when she got back to the mission house late.

But the only thing that mattered was finding Prince.

⌒

"Where on earth is that girl?" Christy murmured as Miss Ida handed her a plate to dry. "It's been half an hour, and it's practically pitch dark out there."

"You know Ruby Mae," Miss Ida said, scrubbing away at a pie tin. "She probably thinks five minutes have gone by. The girl has no sense of time."

"Especially when she's with that horse." Christy set aside her dish towel. "I'd better go get her."

Miss Ida frowned. "What was that? Did you hear something?"

"No, I didn't hear a thing."

"On the front porch. I could have sworn I heard voices."

Christy grinned. "David and the doctor, I'll bet. It's about time!" She grabbed a lamp off the counter and headed for the front door.

Miss Ida followed Christy into the parlor. "Fortunately, there's plenty of pot pie left. I'll just warm it up—"

She was interrupted by a loud, insistent pounding on the door.

"Open up in thar!" came a male voice. "We'uns aim to git in! How 'bout some sweet-heartin', purty ladies?"

Wild, drunken laughter filled the air. Then the voices grew muffled. Christy could hear hoarse whispers. Instantly she doused the light so the men couldn't see inside the house.

She grabbed Miss Ida's arm. "That sounds like Bird's-Eye Taylor," she hissed. "And he's got others with him. Quick, run and be sure the back door is bolted."

Miss Ida dashed back to the kitchen. Her pulse racing, Christy scanned the room. Fortunately, the front door was locked tight, but how long would that last? A strong shoulder could break down that flimsy door. She'd even heard of men shooting hinges right off a door. Could they really do that? And in any case, they could easily break one of the windows if they were determined to get in.

She watched as the brass doorknob slowly turned. "Come on out, little teacher lady," came a slurred voice Christy didn't recognize. "We ain't a-goin' to hurt you."

Again the horrible drunken laughter.

"Plumb feisty, that one is," someone else said. "Citified as they come. Bet she smells mighty fine."

Christy tried to count the different voices. It sounded like three men, but she couldn't be sure. However many there were, they were undoubtedly armed. There was no way that Christy and Miss Ida could fight . . .

Suddenly Christy gasped.

"What is it?" Miss Ida whispered as she rushed back into the parlor.

"Ruby Mae!" Christy cried. "What if she comes back?" She closed her eyes and said a quick, desperate prayer aloud. "Please, God, let Ruby Mae dawdle a little longer."

"Amen to that," Miss Ida whispered. "But Ruby Mae knows what happens when these men are drunk. If she does come back, she'll hear the ruckus and keep her distance."

Someone pounded on the door with what sounded like the butt of a shotgun. "Come on, preacher ladies! We got enough moonshine for all of us to share. Git you likkered up, you'll like it just fine!"

The pounding grew louder. It sounded like all the men were beating on the door at once as they screeched with laughter.

Christy nudged Miss Ida. "The bookcase, quick!"

Together, they struggled to drag the bookcase toward the front door. When it was pulled to within a few inches, Christy paused to wipe her brow. Her mind was racing. How long could they fend off the intruders? If only David or the doctor were here!

"How about the dining room chairs and the piano bench?" Miss Ida hissed.

"Good idea. The bigger the barricade, the better."

"But what if they break through a window?"

Christy paused. "Then we'll protect ourselves."

"With what?" Miss Ida moaned. "Our bare hands?"

"You get the rest of the furniture. I'll worry about our weapons," Christy said with determination.

The voices and pounding grew more insistent. "Come on, gals. We knows yer in thar."

Another voice piped up, "And we knows that nosey preacher's not thar to protect you!"

Christy met Miss Ida's gaze. Even in the near dark, she could see the fear in the older woman's eyes. "How do they know?" Christy asked under her breath.

"Probably saw David on the road," Miss Ida said as she struggled to drag a stuffed chair closer to the door.

Christy ran to the kitchen. She grabbed a cast iron frying pan and a kitchen knife. Back in the parlor, she added two fire pokers to her collection and placed them near the door.

"Our weapons," she whispered to Miss Ida.

Miss Ida reached for one of the frying pans and waved it in the air. "Nothing like a swift whack to the head with one of these," she said.

Christy couldn't help smiling at the prim figure of Miss Ida, thrashing the air ferociously. Christy gave a soft, nervous laugh, and Miss Ida joined in. It helped to break the tension just a little.

"What a pair we make," Miss Ida whispered. "I do hope we live to tell the tale!"

Suddenly the men fell silent. Christy felt her whole body tense. What were they planning? Could they be heading to the back of the house?

"Maybe I should talk to them," Christy whispered.

Miss Ida nodded. "It's worth a try. What have we got to lose?"

Christy cleared her throat. "Who are you, out there?" she called out in a firm, controlled voice.

"It's the purty one!" one of the men cried.

"I hear tell she's feisty as they come, Jubal," another added.

So Jubal McSween was one of the prowlers, Christy

thought. And she was sure she recognized Bird's-Eye's voice. But who was that third man?

"I want you to leave this property right now," Christy said.

"Don't be nervish, now," said Bird's-Eye. "We're not likkered up or nothin'."

"You are, too, liquored up," Miss Ida cried. "And we want you to leave this instant."

"It's the old 'un!" the third man exclaimed. "Poppin' her teeth and carryin' on!"

"Why are you here?" Miss Ida called out. "What is it you men want?"

"Want to teach you'uns a lesson 'bout tellin' us how to live," Jubal said. "Want to give you a taste o' moonshine, change yer minds 'bout it."

"Miss Henderson is going to hear this racket," Christy called. "She'll be over here any minute. I'd advise you to leave quietly, before you get into real trouble. She's a fine shot, you know."

"Aw, she's way over yonder, birthin' a babe," Bird's-Eye said. "You cain't fool us, teacher gal!"

Christy rolled her eyes in frustration. She knew word traveled fast in these mountains, but never before had that fact been a threat to her very life.

"Open up and we'll have ourselves a real play party!" Bird's-Eye called.

"A hullaballoo," Jubal added with a cackle.

Christy glanced over at Miss Ida, who was sitting on the piano bench, her frying pan at the ready.

"There's one thing left to do," Christy whispered.

"What's that? We've run out of furniture and frying pans."

"Pray."

Miss Ida nodded. Together they closed their eyes.

"Please, Lord," Christy whispered, "give us the strength to deal with this crisis. And please, please, keep Ruby Mae out of harm's way—"

The sharp, horrifying clatter of glass breaking stopped Christy in midsentence. Her eyes flew open. On the parlor floor she could just make out the outline of a large rock and shards of glass. Chill air blew in through the broken window.

An arm reached through the hole. "Howdy, ladies," someone said.

"Oh, my Lord," Miss Ida cried in terror. "They're breaking in!"

# Nine

CHRISTY RAISED HER FIRE POKER HIGH AS JUBAL MCSWEEN kicked out the last pieces of glass in the broken window.

"Please, God," Christy prayed, "give me strength."

Suddenly, a white flash of lightning lit up the room. Christy could see the startled look on Jubal's face as he gazed up at the angry sky. A moment later, the whole house shook with the sound of thunder. Windowpanes rattled. The floor shook. It was like nothing Christy had ever heard before.

And then the rain came. It was not the usual spring storm, either. The rain came down in torrents, in buckets, in rivers. A strong wind came with it, driving the rain in horizontal sheets against the windowpanes. It flooded the porch, drenching the men instantly. Puddles formed on the parlor floor as the rain poured in through the broken window.

"Let's git us on inside!" Jubal cried, still standing by the broken window.

Lightening stabbed the sky again. "Dang!" came the voice of the third man. "The still on Blackberry Crik! Crik's a-goin' to flood somethin' fierce. If'n we don't get thar quick, we'll lose the still fer sure!"

A string of curse words followed. Between the blasts of thunder, Christy could hear the men shuffling and muttering on the wooden porch.

Suddenly, the muzzle of a hunting rifle poked through the broken window. A shadowy figure was lit by another burst of lightning. The hate-filled, grizzled face of Bird's-Eye Taylor came into view.

"Another time, preacher ladies," he said with a dark laugh. "I promise you fer sure and certain we'll be back."

The voices vanished, and silence fell over the house. The lightning and thunder quickly faded, and the only sound was the steady drum of the rain on the tin roof.

Christy ran to Miss Ida and hugged her close. "We're safe," Miss Ida whispered, trembling. "We're safe, Christy."

"We are," Christy said grimly. "But Ruby Mae may not be. I'm going to find her."

"But those men—"

"You stay here and wait for David and the doctor. I'll be back before you know it."

"There must be something more I can do," Miss Ida said, wringing her hands.

"Do something about that window," Christy advised. "And pray. It certainly helped just now."

⌐#⟩

"Ruby Mae!" Christy called as she made her way through the woods at the edge of the mission property. By now she'd grown hoarse waiting for an answer.

She had to face the truth. Ruby Mae had run off. Christy

had searched all the mission buildings, hoping Ruby Mae might be hiding from the moonshiners. But after seeing the fence knocked down in the pasture, Christy knew all too well what had happened—Prince had run away, and Ruby Mae had gone to find him.

Christy slogged on through the black forest. The pine-needle floor was soggy, and even with the thick canopy of trees overhead, the rain poured down without mercy. She was soaked to the bone, and her long, wet skirt clung to her legs, making a swift pace impossible.

It wasn't as if she knew where she was going. She knew that Ruby Mae often took Prince down to Blackberry Creek, so that seemed as good a goal as any. But it was just a hunch. Prince could have gone anywhere. David had said the stallion had been acting strangely today. And as for Ruby Mae . . . Well, who knew where she'd have decided to start looking?

There was just one problem with Christy's hunch. She'd heard one of the moonshiners talk about a still on Blackberry Creek. Obviously, she was heading in the same direction they were, and she did not want to run into those men again—especially not all alone in the dark woods. At least in the mission house, she'd felt some tiny bit of security. But out here, with the wind howling and the rain pelting down, she was in their territory. Those men knew these woods in a way she never would. And they were drunk and very angry.

Christy paused to catch her breath near the top of a wide ridge. With her skirts weighed down, she was already exhausted. Her feet were cold, her shoes caked with mud. The icy rain had chilled her to the bone, and she could not stop shivering.

Near as she could tell, Blackberry Creek was down the

steep incline to her left, another quarter mile or so. She could make it that far, then decide her next move. Perhaps she might even find some tracks, although that seemed hard to imagine in this rain.

She started down the ridge. The forest floor was slick, and she had to use trees to support her. Twice she fell. She was climbing to her feet the second time when she heard the unmistakable click of a gun being cocked.

Christy froze. She scanned the darkness, but all she could make out were the dark ghosts of the nearest trees.

"Well, well, well. What have we here? If'n it ain't the teacher gal!" came Bird's-Eye's voice from somewhere to her right. "Lookin' fer us, was you?"

"Changed her mind about the likker, I'll wager!"

She heard the shuffle of feet through leaves and pine needles, and suddenly the men came into view—Bird's-Eye, Jubal, and Duggin Morrison, Ruby Mae's stepfather. So he had been the third man on the porch.

Bird's-Eye came closer. Rain dripped off his felt hat. Christy could smell the sharp tang of tobacco and moonshine. Her stomach lurched.

"Ain't so purty now, is she?" he said. "Looks more like a drowned rat than one of them citified wimmin." He poked at her shoulder with the end of his rifle, but Christy stood tall.

"Let me pass," she said.

The three men hooted. "Let her pass, she says!" Jubal cried. He put a jug to his mouth and guzzled down some liquor.

"Boys, we got business to tend to," Duggin Morrison said.

"The still!" Jubal said, his voice slurred. "I plumb forgot! Let's take the teacher gal with us. We'll make sure the still's all right. Then there'll be plenty o' time for sweetheartin.'"

Bird's-Eye nudged Christy with the barrel of his gun. "Git a move on. We got business by the crik."

With Duggin in the lead, the four of them started down the steep incline. Christy could hear the roar of the swollen creek, not far below them. Bird's-Eye kept his gun trained on her back, poking her along when she stumbled. It was almost impossible for her to keep up, even though they were clearly very drunk.

"Imagine a blossom-eyed gal like her, out in a gully washer storm like this 'un," Jubal said thickly. "Wonder what she were up to."

"Lookin' fer some jollification, I reckon," Bird's-Eye cackled.

"Since you're interested," Christy said, loudly enough to be heard over the steady rain, "I was looking for Ruby Mae Morrison."

Duggin spun around. "I hear you right? Yer a-lookin' for Ruby Mae?"

"She's lost, Mr. Morrison. I think Prince ran off and she's searching for him."

"Aw, don't listen to her, Duggin," Jubal said, taking another swig from his jug. "She's just a-pullin' yer leg."

"It's true, Mr. Morrison," Christy said. "I swear it is."

Duggin paused for a moment, stroking his long beard. "Could be, I reckon. Ruby Mae do love that preacher horse somethin' fierce."

"That stepdaughter of yers is as twitter-witted as they comes," Bird's-Eye said. "Wouldn't be a-tall surprised if she's wanderin' round in the dark lookin' for some no-tailed horse!"

A few feet below them, Blackberry Creek rushed furiously.

Duggin paused near the bank, scratching his head.

"You say she run off tonight?" he asked Christy.

"Quit yer frettin' over that no-good gal," Bird's-Eye snapped. "Ruby Mae ain't been nothin' but trouble and woes fer you since the day she first took breath and squalled. Ain't never shut up since, neither."

"Spring's swolled up somethin' fierce," Duggin said softly. "Ruby Mae told me and her ma she come down here with that preacher horse. Said she liked to think thoughts."

"Actual thoughts," Christy said with an affectionate smile.

"Ruby Mae Morrison?" Bird's-Eye scoffed. "Much as I hate to admit it, the gal can ride. But think? Ain't likely." He poked Christy hard with his gun barrel. "Git movin', teacher gal."

Just then Christy gasped, but it wasn't because of Bird's-Eye's threat. She pointed a trembling finger at a bush near the creek's edge.

A swatch of yellow cloth was caught on one of the branches overhanging the rushing creek.

"That piece of fabric," Christy cried. "That's from Ruby Mae's skirt!"

## *Ten*

DUGGIN KNELT BY THE BANK AND GRABBED THE WET FAB-ric. "It's Ruby Mae's, all right. Her ma made this skirt fer her last Christmas."

Christy stared at the raging creek. She knew Duggin was thinking the same thing she was. What if Ruby Mae had fallen in? What if she had drowned? And if she hadn't fallen in, where was she?

"Ruby Mae!" Duggin called out. "Ruby Mae! Is you here, gal?"

Bird's-Eye cocked his gun again. "We got better things to worry about, Duggin. That gal o' yers is fine. She's a tough 'un. Now, let's git to where we're a-goin'."

Duggin stood slowly, his own gun pointed directly at Bird's-Eye's chest. "I'll tell you where we're goin'," he said fiercely. "We're lookin' fer my Ruby Mae."

The two men stood a few feet apart, their guns trained on each other. Christy shuddered. One wrong word, and those guns could go off. That was the way of Cutter Gap.

"Mr. Taylor," Christy said gently. "What if Lundy were lost right now, instead of Ruby Mae?"

"My boy ain't that stupid."

Duggin answered by cocking his gun.

"Maybe I don't understand much about these mountains," Christy said, her voice trembling, "but I do know one thing: family counts more than anything here. Isn't that true, Bird's-Eye?"

Bird's-Eye took a long, slow breath. His mouth twitched, but he didn't answer.

"Send Jubal to check the still," Christy urged. "You and Duggin and I will look for Ruby Mae."

Bird's-Eye blinked at her in disbelief. "You even know what a still is, teacher gal?"

"I know."

"Well, I never. Cain't say as I thought I'd ever hear such words from the likes of you."

"Neither did I," Christy admitted.

Bird's-Eye jerked his head at Jubal. "Do what the teacher gal says and go check the still. Duggin and me'll go searchin' for that dang-fool stepdaughter o' his."

"What about her?" Jubal demanded, pointing to Christy.

"Her, we'll deal with another day. Blood ties come first in these parts. Teacher gal's got that much right, at least."

With a sigh, Jubal headed off, weaving and swaying along the muddy bank.

"Now what?" Duggin asked. "She could be anywheres. Even . . . " He stared at the raging water mutely.

"You know, Ruby Mae told me once about a cave she goes to near this creek," Christy recalled. "Do you know where it is?"

"Sure," Duggin said. "Just down a ways yonder, on the other side o' the crik."

"It's worth a try," Christy said. "Maybe she went there with Prince to take shelter from the rain."

Christy followed Duggin and Bird's-Eye along the bank. The rain was still coming down hard, and it was difficult to keep up with them. For two men who'd consumed a great deal of moonshine, they were surprisingly nimble.

After a couple hundred yards, Duggin paused. "Cain't see that cave from here, but it's over yonder, behind that brush."

"Ruby Mae!" Christy called. Duggin and Bird's-Eye joined in. After a few moments, they paused to listen.

"Ain't in that cave, I'm afeared," Bird's-Eye said at last. "We're yellin' loud enough to wake the dead."

"You haven't seen Ruby Mae sleep," Christy said.

"True enough," Duggin agreed. "Gal can snore somethin' fierce."

"I'll go see," Christy said.

"Ain't no way yer a-crossin' that crik," Duggin said. "I'm her pa. I'm a-goin'."

"Duggin, you old coot," Bird's-Eye said. "Yer older than the hills. I'll go. 'Sides, yer drunker'n I am."

Duggin cocked his gun again. "Old coot, ya say?"

"Mr. Morrison," Christy said, pushing away the gun. "We don't have time for this."

Duggin hung his head. "Yer right. And so is Bird's-Eye, I'm afeared."

Bird's-Eye handed Duggin his gun. "Here goes nothin'," he said.

Slowly Bird's-Eye made his way across the raging creek. Halfway across, the water came all the way to his chest.

"Careful, you mean old buzzard," Duggin called.

They watched as Bird's-Eye crawled back up the far bank and disappeared into the brush, where the cave was hidden.

"Mr. Morrison?" Christy said.

"Yep?"

"Are you the one who shaved Prince?"

The old man paused. "Naw. Jubal did that. Me, I ain't never seen any point in pickin' on critters. It's men I got my feudin' with." He shrugged. "'Sides, I would never a done somethin' to hurt Ruby Mae that way."

"Maybe you should tell her that," Christy said. "When we find her."

"If'n we find her."

They heard Bird's-Eye's cry from the far bank.

"Ya think?" Duggin asked hopefully.

A moment later, the thick brush parted to reveal a sleepy-eyed Ruby Mae on Prince's back. Bird's-Eye came running out behind them.

"Sound asleep they was, in the cave, snorin' away just like you said!" he called.

"Miz Christy?" Ruby Mae yelled. "Pa? What're you doin' out here in the rain? You're soaked to the bone!"

"Come on, Ruby Mae," Bird's-Eye said loudly, "yer goin' straight back to the mission where you cain't get into any more trouble."

Christy looked over at Duggin. "Are we?" she asked. "Going back to the mission, I mean?"

Duggin nodded. "I reckon so."

He went to the edge of the bank, waiting for Bird's-Eye to return Ruby Mae safely. Christy thought she saw him wipe away a tear. Of course, she realized after a moment, it might just have been a drop of rain. After all, there was no telling what was going on in the hearts of these mountain men. Not long ago, they'd had her fearing for her life. Now, she didn't know whether to fear them . . . or pity them.

Maybe, she thought sadly, that's how it would always be.

⌐#⌐

Late that night, Christy sat by the fire in the mission house. Everyone had long since gone to bed. Only she and Dr. Mac-Neill were still awake.

"If only I hadn't left," the doctor said for the hundredth time. "None of this might ever have happened. If you hadn't sent David to fetch me, if the rain hadn't slowed down our return . . ."

"Ifs," Christy said as she watched the embers in the fire-place glow. "There's no point in doing this again, Neil. Everything turned out fine."

"This time," the doctor said darkly.

"I feel badly, too, actually," Christy admitted. "I wanted David to bring you back here because of your fever, but getting soaked in that rain couldn't have helped you any."

The doctor smiled. "Come to think of it, I am feeling a bit light headed. Could be delirium setting in."

Christy reached over to feel his forehead. "You do feel hot."

"Strangest thing. I'm hearing music too. Think I'm hallucinating?" He stood, grinning down at her, and reached out his hand. "You do still owe me a dance, you know."

"Now that you mention it," Christy said as she got to her feet, "I seem to be hearing music too."

She gave a little curtsy and the doctor pulled her close,

using his good arm. Together, they swept slowly around the parlor, dancing to the music of the rain drumming on the roof.

"I'm so glad you're all right," the doctor whispered.

Christy lay her head on his broad chest. Memories whirled in her mind—frightening memories. The doctor's blood-soaked shirt. The sound of the parlor window shattering. The cold muzzle of Bird's-Eye's gun between her shoulders.

She closed her eyes. The doctor was humming an old mountain tune. The fire crackled softly.

Slowly, one by one, other memories came to her. Miss Alice's graceful smile at her birthday party. Starlight spilling over Prince's coat that night in the shed. Ruby Mae's musical laughter. Christy's class at recess, filled with high spirits and spring fever—filled with love for these beautiful, dangerous, complicated, God-given mountains.

The doctor paused. "What are you thinking?" he asked.

"I was thinking," Christy whispered, "that I don't want this dance to ever end."

# *About Catherine Marshall*

**Catherine Marshall LeSourd** (1914–1983), a *New York Times* bestselling author, is best known for her novel *Christy*. Based on the life of her mother, a teacher of mountain children in poverty-stricken Tennessee, *Christy* captured the hearts of millions and became a popular CBS television series. As her mother reminisced around the kitchen table at Evergreen Farm, Catherine probed for details and insights into the rugged lives of these Appalachian highlanders.

The Christy® of Cutter Gap series, based on the characters of the beloved novel, contains expanded adventures filled with romance, excitement, and intrigue.

Catherine also wrote *Julie*, a sweeping novel of love and adventure, courage and commitment, tragedy and triumph, in a Pennsylvania steel town during the Great Depression.

Catherine's first husband, Peter Marshall, was Chaplain of the U.S. Senate, and her intimate biography of him, *A Man Called Peter*, became an international bestseller and Academy Award Nominated movie. The story shares the power of this dynamic man's love for his God and for the woman he married.

A beloved inspirational writer and speaker, Catherine's enduring career spanned four decades and six continents, and reached over 30 million readers.

# CHRISTY'S ADVENTURES CONTINUE IN...

Christy should be thrilled when David, the handsome minister, proposes marriage. So why do thoughts of Dr. Neil MacNeill keep popping into her head?

Before she can answer David, Christy is blinded in a terrible riding accident and all her dreams are threatened.

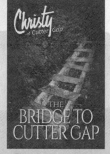

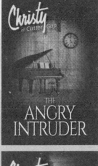

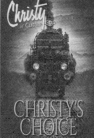

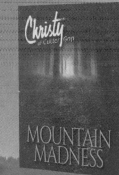